The Fifth Di...
December 2024

Features
- 60   Article: Speculative Fiction and Cultural Identity by Yuliia Vereta
- 112 Who's Who

Short Stories
- 6   The Hydrogen Barrier by Gustavo Bondoni
- 27   On Board the U.S.S. Somoza by Alan Ira Gordon
- 46   Sky Shrieks by David Castlewitz
- 65   Helios by Zachary Grant
- 83   The Last Unicorn by Lisa Voorhees
- 96   Music Appreciation by Lindsey Duncan

Poetry
- 23   what say by Denise Noe
- 26   planetary conformity by Lee Clark Zumpe
- 44   Listening to Dandelions by George Anthony Kulz
- 57   A Century Divides Us by Lee Clark Zumpe

Helios by Zachary Grant was originally published by Altered Reality Magazine in 2024.

THE STAFF OF THE FIFTH DI...:

EDITOR: Tyree Campbell
WEBMASTER: H David Blalock
COVER DESIGNERS: Laura Givens; Marcia A. Borell

Cover art "Cruisin'" by Laura Givens
Cover design by Laura Givens

Vol. V, No.3   December 2024

The Fifth Di... is published three times a year on the 1st day of April, August, and December in the United States of America by Hiraeth Publishing, P.O. Box 1248, Tularosa, NM, 88352. Copyright 2024 by Hiraeth Publishing. All rights revert to authors and artists upon publication except as noted in selected individual contracts. Nothing may be reproduced in whole or in part without written permission from the authors and artists. Any similarity between places and persons mentioned in the fiction or semi-fiction and real places or persons living or dead is coincidental. Writers and artists guidelines are available online at www.hiraethsffh.com. Guidelines are also available upon request from Hiraeth Publishing, P.O. Box 1248, Tularosa, NM, 88352, if request is accompanied by a self-addressed #10 envelope with a first-class US stamp. Editor: Tyree Campbell.

A Little Help, Please

In the world of the small indie press we fight a never-ending battle for attention to our work, as writers and in publishing. Here's an example: big publishers [you know who they are] have gobs of $$$ that they can devote to advertising and marketing. Here at Hiraeth Publishing, our advertising budget consists of the deposits for whatever soda bottles and aluminum cans we can find alongside the highways. Anti-littering laws make our task even more difficult . . . ☺

That's where YOU come in. YOU are our best promoter. YOU are the one who can tell others about us. Just send 'em to our website, tell them about our store. That's all. Just that.

Of course, we don't mind if you talk us up. We're pretty good, you know. We have some award-winning and award-nominated writers and artists, plus other voices well-deserving to be heard [not everyone wins awards, right?] but our publications are read-worthy nevertheless.

That number once again is:
www.hiraethsffh.com

Friend us on Facebook at Hiraeth Publishing
Follow us on Twitter at @HiraethPublish1

Pevely Keiser in:
THE IPHAJEAN LARK

Five hundred years into the future, Pevely Keiser is the capo of the criminal organization called Temmen. Temmen runs itself, for the most part, with only a few nudges from Pevely to keep people in line. Lately she has two things on her mind. She wants to do something good and useful with the funds that accrue to the gang. And she wants a companion or two to help her…and perhaps to share her bed, for she well knows it's lonely at the top.

In the process of training her two new assistants (and possible companions) Pevely comes across a young woman being chased. Taking her on board, Pevely soon learns of a devastating conspiracy that threatens the Confederation with totalitarian rule. The key to the solution lies in the hands of one of her employees, but is it the right key? Only the corporate hierarch who leads the conspiracy knows for sure. And he is the father of the woman Pevely rescued.

https://www.hiraethsffh.com/product-page/iphajean-lark-by-tyree-campbell

The Hydrogen Barrier
Gustavo Bondoni

"Thank you Mr. Verstappen."

The printout slid over the dark, polished wood of the desk – de Souza's way of indicating that the meeting was over. No words of encouragement, no praise, despite being on time and under budget.

Jerry Verstappen hadn't been expecting anything of the sort anyway. The printout, details of an international bank transfer, had the right number on it. The bonus for early completion of the stage was correctly calculated, and it had been wired to the correct Swiss account – something he already knew because he'd gotten an email over his satellite message service. The money was in the bank, and that was what mattered.

The meeting had gone well enough; there was no way to make everyone happy. If they did a good job, he would be stepping on the toes of the government faction that wanted a new supplier to come in, which would mean kickbacks for them. If they fell even one day behind, the media would stir the population into a frenzy, demanding that the government rescind their contract and freeze their assets. Underlying that was a feeling of hurt national pride. The technology to do this was available, so why couldn't the job be done by a Brazilian company instead of calling in outsiders? After all, didn't the mere existence of the project mean that Brazil was one of the true first-world countries, an economic power?

Well, if Brazil had really been first-world, they'd have broken the hydrogen barrier before now. After all, hadn't every other important industrialized country done so?

Jerry smiled to himself as he left the building. The government had already been burned by trusting local contractors – twice! – and had wisely decided to swallow their pride. It took a special kind of company to run a project like this one, and, despite the international uproar that the hiring had caused, Verstappen's company was one of the few that could guarantee results. If Brazil wasn't up to Standard in six months he would forego half his fee.

He walked calmly along the beach. Rio was still one of the most dangerous cities in the world, and dusk was the deadliest hour, a time when tourists were still about, cursed with a false sense of security in the failing light.

Verstappen had witnessed one purse-snatching and one armed robbery during his walks, but had yet to be approached himself despite his light blond hair and pale skin, which marked him as a foreigner of some kind. Despite the fact that he wore a watch worth ten years' salary for a Brazilian where everyone could see it. There was something about the way he walked that warned the scum away. Or maybe it was just that he was six foot seven and built like a brick wall.

Either way, he knew they would come eventually, and he hoped they came with knives. That way, he would get to go hand-to-hand. Shooting people was so impersonal – even if, in the end, the result was the same.

He had no luck that day, arriving at his company's base without incident.

Headquarters was the first floor of a luxury hotel overlooking the water on Copacabana. He tossed his sport jacket to a valet and headed for the terrace, where he'd find most of his crew at this hour. The valet was a government spy, and the contents of the pockets would be photographed and analyzed before the garment was returned, but he didn't care. He'd been completely upfront with his employers, and, besides, it would be hot on the terrace bar. He wasn't in the mood to carry the thing around.

Francois spotted him as soon as he entered, and waved him over. It was an amazing display from the small dark mulatto: no matter how much alcohol he'd consumed, or how distracted he ought to be, the guy always knew exactly what was going on around him.

Verstappen judged that he should have been very distracted. He had a pretty blonde in a bikini sitting on each knee, both evidently drunk as sailors on shore leave. One of them had her hand on his crotch while the other had her tongue in his ear, one nipple peering unnoticed from the displaced bra. Yet Francois noted his employer's entrance and waved him over. Nothing got past him, and that was why he was head of Verstappen International's field operations.

As Jerry approached, the other man stood, displacing both women, and extended a hand. Verstappen shook it and sat down, glancing meaningfully at the girls.

"My sweets," Francois said to them, "I'm afraid I have some business to attend to. Why don't you wait for me in my room, it's number 109 – help yourselves to anything in the bar – I ordered champagne."

They left, squealing with delight which rang a little false to Jerry. He looked after them. "Spies?" he said.

Francois took a drink. "One of them is, for sure. She spilt half of everything she drank and acted a lot more drunk than she should have been even if she'd drunk what she pretended to. And, every once in a while an intelligent question came through the bimbo act. The other... I'm not sure, I think she's just a whore the government put up to make the 'two drunken sluts' routine credible. One thing's for sure, though."

Verstappen raised his eyebrows letting the other man continue.

"They're going to earn every penny of their salaries tonight!" he leered.

Jerry rolled his eyes. He knew they would: Francois liked it often and he liked it rough, and liked it best when someone else was footing the bill. "You needed something?"

"Yeah. There's a little bit of a problem in Sao José." Sao José was a small city about an hour from Sao Paulo notable only because it held a number of plants belonging to international companies whose worldwide operations forced them to follow the Standard a little less strictly than they might have otherwise.

"Problem?"

"The mayor. He wants his cousin's construction company to get the job of laying the hydrogen lines for the gas stations. And he claims it's at least a hundred-million dollar job, wink-wink. He won't sign our operating permit, otherwise."

Typical South American administration, but it could put a crimp in their project timeline if not dealt with quickly.

Jerry knew the request would have been denied out of hand, and that an alternative offer would have been made.

"How high was his bribe request when we told him no?"

"Over budget."

"When do you think the problem will be solved?"

"Well, we have a couple of other documents signed by this same man, which means his signature is familiar to our people, so I'm guessing that it will be a non-issue by ten o'clock at night."

"Good." Jerry flagged down a passing waiter and ordered a Caipirinha with lots of sugar. They drank in silence for a few minutes until Francois, finishing his drink, excused himself.

"Have some business waiting, hope you don't mind," he said.

Jerry nodded. "Do you think the spy might have a friend or two around here?"

The mulatto laughed, but responded. "Try the girl on the second stool in the bar. Have fun."

Jerry, turned to see where the other man had pointed. The girl was definitely a good-looking woman, with long, dark hair, but seemed to show no interest whatsoever in any of the people at the bar. Just having a drink and a chat with what appeared to be her mother.

"Are you sure?"

Francois winked. "Trust me."

Verstappen picked up his drink and headed over, deep misgivings in his heart. If Francois was right, he would be getting a bonus in his next paycheck.

***

The intendente's house and his security were well thought out. Tall walls, infrared cameras and at least six guards – four on the grounds and two more inside – should have been enough to keep the mayor and his sleeping family safe.

As a matter of fact, it should have insured that no attempt was even made on the house. This was San José Dos Campos, after all, not Rio or Sao Paulo. In either of those cities, you could expect ambitious assaults by helicopter-mounted, machine-gun-toting criminals, but not here. This was a small industrial town where human predators only fed off the weak and poorly guarded.

Mercedes Lopez smiled, tied her hair back with a rubber band, and donned a black balaclava. The guards were probably not expecting trouble. Even if they had, private security guards were no match for her team, tempered by combat in fields all over the globe – from Afghanistan to Colombia, and from Somalia to Sri Lanka. Her troops had little in common – some had been professional soldiers while others had been revolutionaries, or terrorists – except that each was among the best at what he or she did. And all of them had renounced ideals and military discipline for corporate life of a sort that paid extremely well.

They were ready to go. They'd been ready for the past half hour, but Mercedes had made them wait patiently for a cloudbank to obscure the moon, turning what had been a bright night a little darker.

There. The darkness complete, she placed her night vision goggles in front of her eyes, identified Salenko and signaled for him to begin.

They'd discussed the plan at length, tossing different solutions back and forth between them, before deciding that the situation really didn't call for anything all that fancy. The house was nearly ten miles from town and half a mile from the nearest house. This meant that, even if they were heard, help wouldn't arrive in time to stop anything.

They'd decided on a direct assault.

The security camera on this side was mounted too high to try to cut the wires or paint over the lens, so it would have to be shot out. In Lopez's opinion, this was the riskiest part of the operation. Salenko's silenced Steyr sniper rifle was the only weapon in their arsenal that hadn't been "liberated" from a group of Rio-based druglords – hard, well-prepared men who hadn't been expecting a raid by a mercenary special-ops group. If the ballistics people analyzed that single round, questions might be asked.

But with the amount of shooting coming, she really doubted the police would bother with that one bullet two stories up.

A soft whoosh to her left told her that the shot had been taken, and the clatter ahead, that it had made contact. While it was impossible to verify if the camera had been destroyed, she knew Salenko. He hadn't missed.

Another man broke cover. He walked calmly to a point forty meters ahead of the front gate, a solid oaken affair, lifted a metal tube to his shoulder and fired off a small antitank missile. The gate exploded into matchsticks with a loud boom.

That was their cue. The guards would all be rushing in this direction, and everyone inside the house would be awake, wondering what the hell was going on. Time to move.

The team ran through the opening and spread out. The only guard in evidence was unconscious next to the opening, bleeding profusely from multiple shrapnel wounds. They ignored him, except to remove his weapons. His companions would be arriving at any moment.

Mercedes led four members of her team towards the house itself, having no trouble finding cover in the heavily wooded grounds. The house guards, she found, had made a big mistake. One of them was perched, pistol in hand behind an open first floor window. Although the room behind him had been darkened to avoid detection, his heat signature would have been visible from the moon. All four Kalashnikovs opened fire, and the man disappeared from sight.

"The other one is probably in the surveillance room," Lopez whispered. "Karl, go after him. Joao, I need you to take the women."

The men nodded, and the team sprinted forward. The bay windows on the ground floor dissolved in a spray of machine-gun fire and they were in.

Mercedes sprinted up the stairs, to where their study of the house showed the master bedroom was located. She made the landing just as the door opened, and a man who was hurriedly tying a bathrobe emerged and started bellowing for an explanation what the hell was going on, in Portuguese.

He never knew what hit him. Before he had time to find a light switch, a burst from Mercedes' gun tore him in half and he fell to the floor.

Mission accomplished, she thought grimly. Now, everything depended on Joao. If the wife came out of the bedroom before he arrived, she would have to die. There was no other choice.

Mercedes lay in the dark and waited. The woman in the darkened room was timidly asking what was going on, but the soft questions quickly became hysterical screams when her husband failed to reply. Mercedes could see her approaching the open doorway and tensed, ready to fire.

Footsteps in the corridor alerted her that someone was coming. Two clicks on her radio told her it was Joao. She clicked back, once, and he moved. He stormed into the room, screamed at the woman in Portuguese and forced her to the floor. Inside of ten seconds, she'd been chloroformed and had stopped struggling. Mercedes entered the room.

"The girls?" she whispered.

"They're all right. Gonna have a hell of a headache in the morning. They heard me, though, loud and clear. They'll tell the police that their attacker was Brazilian, Carioca."

"Good. Let's find the safe, steal some jewelry and get the fuck out of here."

Gunfire in other parts of the dark house told her that the rest of her team was still on the job.

***

A few miles away, a solitary man went through a third story window in a government building. Unlike Mercedes, his entry would have to go completely unnoticed and unsuspected. Which was why the maid he'd bribed to leave this window open was already on her way to the slave pens in Sudan. He loved working in Latin America. Where else would a government building have wood-framed windows that opened with little brass handles? He was more used to having to deal with intelligent security systems and grids of laser light.

His job was simple. All he had to do was place a single envelope in the day's outgoing mail, which would then be picked up the following morning. An envelope that contained a single, signed authorization.

***

The Brazilian press had gathered en masse. These weekly press conferences, whose original attendance had consisted exclusively of economic beat writers, had gradually expanded as the controversy surrounding Brazil's move from traditional energy sources to the Hydrogen-based Kyoto Standard had increased. The controversy had grown in steps.

The first step had been inevitable. Someone within the government had leaked the information regarding Verstappen International's fee. And the additional nugget that the enormous fee was only for managing the project, and for getting it done on time. Construction, materials, logistics, and everything else were included in an estimate, annexed to the back of the proposal. Verstappen knew the estimate was accurate, and his reputation was partly based on the fact that he'd never gone more than ten percent over estimate, but in this land of corruption, no one would ever believe it.

The second step had come when, during the building of a new hydroelectric facility at the Amazon, his workers had been threatened by machete-wielding tree-huggers – who, in light of their excessive blondness and foreign accents were unlikely to have been from Brazil – who claimed to represent the dozens of tribes of unassimilated natives that would be displaced by the rising waters. Heated words had been exchanged between the protesters and the security team until one of the protesters, convinced that public opinion would protect the righteous against anything, took a swing at one of the guards, inspiring the rest of the protesters to surge forward. The only thing they didn't take into consideration was that this security force wasn't made up of trembling security guards or corporate spokesmen. It was made up of well-armed elite former soldiers who knew exactly what to do when attacked by a mob with machetes. The international outcry following the massacre had been enormous. And ignored by both Verstappen and the government.

After that, the conferences were filled with ever more and ever more aggressive journalists. TV cameras became omnipresent. But things didn't come to a head until three months later. On one Saturday in June, the Chinese government announced that they had made Standard. Inspection teams confirmed this two weeks later, and Brazil's economy began to teeter. China was their biggest customer, and, in order to stay on Standard, a certain percentage of their imports would have to come from compliant nations. The cutbacks in Brazilian production had already begun, but it was impossible for a country of nearly four hundred million to simply cut its production levels by a third. The result would be unemployment, rising poverty and, eventually, complete social chaos.

Suddenly, what had begun as another way to laugh at the government's stupidity changed completely. Suddenly, it became important. The questions became more and more relevant and intelligent, and small peccadilloes more likely to be overlooked.

Verstappen faced the crowd and calmly concluded his status report – essentially saying that everything was ahead of schedule and under budget, and that Brazil would be on Standard within the next six months. "I will now field any questions you might have," he said.

The first reporter to raise his micro-recording unit was from a sensationalist rag based in Río. A typical scandals and conspiracy-theory piece of crap that had adapted magnificently to the internet age by reprinting everything it found on the sites of its European counterparts, and giving those same counterparts as impeccable references. Their readers were, of course, insufficiently educated to spot it.

Verstappen knew what was coming, yet acknowledged her immediately.

"Mr. Verstappen, do you have any comment regarding the death of the Mayor of Sao Jose Dos Campos last night?"

"Yes. I heard about it this morning. A tragic affair. I'd like to send my condolences to his wife and daughters."

"You say it's tragic, but it seems to me that you've been very lucky lately. Everyone who opposes the project or raises concerns about the legality of what you've been doing seems to suffer either a setback, an accident, or, as in this case, a tragic robbery."

"We initially had some differences with Mr. Cardoso, but we eventually smoothed them over. As a matter of fact, he signed our permits yesterday. He wasn't standing in our way at all. He was a firm and helpful ally who was concerned with the well-being of his city. Once we put those concerns to rest, he no longer opposed our plan."

After that, the rest of the questions were a breeze.

***

The transforming station was deep in the Amazon, about a hundred miles west of the nearest town, Gurupi. Electricity from the hydro plants further up the river would be shunted to the main power grid north of Brasilia here in this concrete bunker. It also seemed like most of the red mud from the surrounding area had been tracked onto the floor of the office by members of the team.

Verstappen would have preferred to keep running things from the comfort of the hotel but, sometimes, when things happened, it was necessary to get one's hands dirty – or, in this particular case, one's feet.

The hitch occurred when eight of the local workers, not really much more than prehistoric villagers hired to shore up the banks of the river were killed when the surface they were working on was undermined by a sudden surge in the water level. This would normally have been considered a cost of doing business, but the press had discovered that the surge had been caused by tests of the dam's gates upriver. A dam which had been built, and was being tested, by Vertappen's people.

Work at the site had ground to a halt and Verstappen, deciding to make a PR success out of the disaster, had boarded the first available helicopter with Francois and Mercedes, and was soon on site. The briefing by the station manager had been brief, professional and to the point.

"We can't do a thing. The damned natives are picketing us peacefully, but effectively enough that new workers can't get through. The local sheriff isn't willing to help because his brother was one of the men killed in the slide, and we can't get rid of the protesters ourselves due to the presence of the TV crews."

"The men who were killed, did they have families?" Verstappen asked.

"Most of them were married, and four of them had children."

"Have we offered compensation packages?"

"Of course, the standard. And they say that they want the packages, but they also want help from the government to make their town live again. Nearly every able-bodied man in the village was killed."

"Not much of a village, was it?"

"Fifty or sixty people. Most of them old men, women and children. The younger men have been moving to the city to find work."

"How does a village like that survive, anyway?"

"Very precariously, it seems. The problem is that now, they claim that we've destroyed their village and their way of life, and that no matter what we offer them, we can't give that back."

"We'll just have to see about that, won't we? Can you take me to the picket leaders?"

"Right away, sir."

***

The manager had been right about the age of the villagers.

As the group approached, Verstappen could see that none of the men on the picket line looked less than fifty, and even those relatively young men moved with the cautious slowness of people decades their senior. The majority of the picket was made up of women.

The sun shone down on them, and Jerry wondered how it could be that, despite the constant sunshine, they were walking through knee-deep mud. Between heat, humidity and mud, it seemed to take an eternity to reach the picket line.

Verstappen walked in the lead. This group didn't seem likely to become violent, and it would be great PR for the project when they aired the tapes of this meeting on the news tonight: he wasn't just a figurehead who appeared when there was good news to be relayed. He was also there when things went wrong, when an unexpected tragedy on his watch hurt a community. And not only was he there to face the consequences, he was out front, trying to find a way to heal terrible wounds. It would be brilliant.

As he approached the group, he spotted a little girl among them. She looked about what one would expect from a ten-year-old Amazonian: slightly Mongoloid features, a bony frame covered in chocolate-milk colored skin. She wasn't acting like one, however. A little boy was trying to get her to play what looked like a variation of tag and, every once in a while, he would succeed in getting her to take a couple of desultory running steps after him. But then she would slow to a walk, and then halt and look towards the river.

Jerry watched them play this scenario out several times as the Verstappen International group approached the villagers. When they were less than ten meters from the main body of adults, the boy did it again. He tagged her and ran straight towards the foreigners, but peeled off with a frightened shriek when he saw the group sloshing through the mud and ran back to the safety of the group behind him.

The little girl, on the other hand, simply halted a few meters ahead of Verstappen, completely ignoring both the adults and the boy as she stared blankly towards the river. There were no tears, but Jerry could see that her eyes were red-rimmed and crusted from what had come before.

He knelt in the mud a meter in front of her. She turned to gaze at him. There was no fear in her eyes, just puzzlement as she seemed to take him in with her small, deep brown eyes, and to weigh him in her head. "Are you the man who killed my daddy?" she asked, in Portuguese, seemingly unsure whether to be accusing or afraid.

"No, dear," he replied. "Your daddy was killed in an accident. It was a sad thing, but it wasn't really anyone's fault."

"That's not what Henrique says."

"Can you show me Henrique?"

The little girl pointed towards the picket leaders standing a few feet away. Henrique seemed to be the only youngish member of the group – a man who definitely should have been among the dead. Verstappen got out of the mud and, pausing only to extend a hand which the little girl hesitantly took, walked towards the villagers.

"It saddens me that you would make a little girl believe something like that," he said.

Henrique withered under the other's blue-eyed gaze, involuntarily taking one step back. But he still had the courage to respond. "It's always the same," he spat.

"Gringos come in and make money from the jungle – they don't care if a few Indians die."

Verstappen felt a flash of anger – more from the fact that this peasant had dared talk back to him than because what he was saying was untrue – but kept it in check for the sake of the newsmen. "What happened here was an unfortunate accident. We will reimburse the families of the dead. Not because we think that will take away the pain, but because it is the only thing we can do now. We truly care about the well-being of our workers, and, in order to show it, we will also build a new schoolhouse for the village. With the new station here, your village will prosper beyond anything you've seen before. And this little girl here will be able to have access to the best education in Brazil."

Emboldened by Verstappen's appeasing demeanor, Henrique snorted. "Maia won't get an education at all. She'll be lucky to survive the winter – both her father and uncle were killed in the flood, and her mother was already dead. Do you really think anyone else in the village will want to take her in? That child is cursed by the jungle." He made a sign with his hands – a warding gesture.

His face never showed anything but concern, but, inwardly, Verstappen smiled. He had them. "I can't allow that. Maia will return with us, and be privately schooled. I will personally pay for her education until she graduates from university. And she will be cared for by the best nannies I can get in Rio until I can find her a foster family." Verstappen turned his back on the crowd, who knew they'd lost the edge, and, as he passed the manager gave him a meaningful look. "I've done my bit," he hissed, audible only to the manager and the little girl who, presumably, knew no English. "Now get this thing back the fuck on schedule."

The manager swallowed and nodded.

***

"We are very pleased, Mr. Verstappen. Our government has decided to make you an offer for the final phase of the project. Despite the fact some people feel that the conversion to hydrogen has advanced far enough that it can be completed by Brazilian companies now, we have no wish to risk delays on the certification side," De Souza said, handing him a printout.

Jerry looked over the terms and part of him was stunned. It was obvious that the Brazilians were very pleased at the work they'd managed to do so far – the offer was generous beyond his wildest dreams. The rest of him, however, managed to remain in control. Not a flicker of any emotion crossed his features. He gazed impassively into the president's eyes and said, "I'll have to think about it."

They exchanged greetings and he left the office.

Sitting patiently outside, swinging her legs from a chair, he found Maia. She looked up as he approached and gave him a big smile. At first, he'd shown himself spending time with the little girl only for the benefit of the TV cameras but, gradually, her mix of direct innocence and shrewd intelligence had grown on him. He often had her brought to the government offices after her school day was over, and they walked down the beach back to the hotel together, until it had become an end-of-the-day ritual. He'd even arranged things so that he was getting off work earlier – that way, the risk of a robbery would be lessened.

The crew had also adopted the little aboriginal as a kind of mascot. They'd even doubled his bodyguard whenever he walked along the beach with her. They thought he wouldn't notice but, even if they always stayed far enough away that he couldn't see their faces, it was hard to miss the fact that there always seemed to be a couple of European tourists with military bearings a few hundred yards from them.

The warm breeze caressed their faces as they strolled in a leisurely way across the beach, pausing every now and again so that Maia could admire one of the sand sculptures or to try to get him to buy her a necklace off one of the vendor's carts.

Jerry seldom indulged her, since he didn't want her to grow up with no concept of the value of money, but decided to splurge that day. After all, he thought with a smile, I think I can afford it.

Excited by her new treasure, Maia opened up. It was very unusual for her to initiate conversations – the normal course of events was for Verstappen to ask her questions about her day, her teachers, her tests – but today seemed to be an exception in this as well.

"Jerry," she said. It had been a struggle to get her to call him anything but senhor, "can I ask you a question?"

Surprised, he nodded.

"There are some children at school who say that you're just here to steal all the Brazilian money, and that you're just another gringo trying to get rich off of us. Why do they say that?"

Verstappen sighed inwardly. "It's complicated," he began, but then immediately recognized that this girl's intelligence deserved a better answer than a brush-off. "We are working on a big job for the government, and lots of people think that the work should have gone to a Brazilian company."

"And why didn't they give the work to Brazilians? We're in Brazil, after all!" Maia was very proud of the geography she'd learned. "My teacher says that you're from far away. All the way across this sea."

"The problem is that the job has to be done right, and it has to be done quickly. And, sometimes, Brazilian companies take a long time to do things." He decided not to mention the fact that they were corrupt and dishonest, as well. His firm might be even more ruthless than anyone dared print, but the government was getting what they paid for, on time and without questions.

"And what is this thing you're doing?"

"Do you know what hydrogen is?" he asked her.

She shook her head, eyes widening at the big word.

"Hydrogen is a gas – like steam, or air. It can be used to make electricity or to run cars. It's very good for the environment – the land, the trees and the animals. So using hydrogen is necessary to make the Earth a nice place to live. But it's not easy to get, and it's not easy to move, and it's not easy to store. Special factories and pipes and tanks need to be built to use hydrogen to make Brazil a better place." It would have been useless to try to explain that other countries with lots of money weren't going to buy any Brazilian products until it happened – better to explain the environmental root cause.

"So you made Brazil a better place?"

"We're working on it," he said.

She smiled, a child's smile – warm, bright and innocent. "I'm glad you're going to make Brazil a better place."

In the back of his mind, he saw the number on the sheet that De Souza had offered to complete the project, but he also compared it to the bigger number on the contract offer that had come in from India. Essentially, the Indians were desperate. They needed him there now, and had offered a contract an order of magnitude larger to let some Brazilian firm take care of the certification and come help India jumpstart their Hydrogen infrastructure projects.

But his smile hid these things. He tousled her hair affectionately and they walked on.

***

They were on a beach once more, two months later, and Maia was eating an ice-cream cone; it was another warm day, and they had just had lunch. It was one of those rare Fridays on which Verstappen could take an afternoon off, and he had – and treated Maia to a feijao-less meal at a fast-food burger place fronting the beach. To her, a greasy hamburger was heaven. He'd made do with some coffee and a slice of the chain's banana pie.

As far as he could remember, life had never been better. His parents hadn't been rich, and he'd gone straight into the army out of school – and done stints with several of the euphemistically termed "irregular" armies that always seemed so necessary in Africa. It might not have been as respectable as the regular military, but it certainly had paid a whole lot better once his troop had made a name for itself.

Moving on to battlefield engineering had only made things worse, if more profitable. It wasn't fun to be somewhere trying to put up a bridge while others were trying to stop you with machine guns – it tended to make it hard to concentrate. But it had also led to respectability, and they'd made the natural transition and exchanged real sniping for political sniping, although things could still come to violence out in the field. And the political side almost left him yearning for a good pitched battle with another mercenary force.

But all that seemed years away now, as he strolled down the Brazilian beach. The government had paid half of the promised fee up front, and was due to pay the rest on completion of the certification process. It was true that the end was still a few weeks away, but what was left mainly involved negotiating with the Kyoto Standard inspectors, who were honest if strict. He didn't really need to be involved, and was starting to enjoy being nothing but a figurehead.

Suddenly he felt an impact on his left shoulder as if an invisible fist had struck him out of thin air. Tiny droplets of liquid sprayed over his face. He stood there, shocked for a moment until the pain hit him and he realized that he'd just been shot.

His training immediately took over – he dropped to the floor. It urged him to find cover right now, and identified two potential places of concealment nearby: a slight dune straight ahead and a wooden drink stand to his left.

He was about to dive behind the stand when another bullet whistled overhead brought him back to reality. Maia had walked ahead and was standing on top of the slight dune, just now realizing he wasn't with her. She turned to see what was holding him back, and seemed more surprised than frightened to see him lying on the sand.

Up there on the dune, she was silhouetted against the sky. A perfect target for the shooter.

He ignored everything he'd ever been taught, got back up and ran for the dune. He tackled the little girl, who immediately began to cry in fear. He ignored her, and put his body between Maia and the place he thought the shots were coming from. And he lay there for what seemed like an eternity but was more likely thirty seconds, listening to a gunfight that began – he assumed his bodyguards, never too far behind, had identified the shooter and were laying down suppressing fire.

The shots ended as quickly as they'd begun. After a minute of silence, he risked looking up to see what the situation was. His shoulder was killing him, but he had to push the pain out of the way for now.

Francois was walking along the beach holding the Glock he preferred when out with the bodyguards. He gave Verstappen's shoulder a cursory glance and, seeing that the wound was not life threatening, made a face. "I suppose you couldn't find anywhere more exposed to lay down while being shot at? You're lucky he decided to try to take you near the hotel, and we were all over him in seconds."

"I am a bit visible, aren't I?" Jerry replied, grimacing through the pain. But he had to ignore it just a little while longer. There were things he had to know. "Who was it?"

"Local tough. Not much of a marksman, either. Again, your luck seems to hold."

"Did you take him alive?"

Francois looked hurt. "Of course. I, unlike certain other people I could name, do not disregard all of my training when someone starts shooting."

"And?"

"Pictures of you in his cell phone. It was a contract killing. I told you the Indians wouldn't be happy with your refusal. They really need to beat Brazil to the certification."

"Yeah, I guess you were right. But you understand I had to do it."

Francois was about to make another snide remark, but he stopped, looked at the exposed position on top of the dune, looked at the girl, now silent, but with her sand-covered face streaked with tears, and he sighed. "Yeah, I guess I do. Who'd have thought it? The ambulance is on its way," he said, and then switched to Portuguese, for Maia's benefit. "And let's get you another ice cream cone."

Maia smiled.

what say
Denise Noe

omen – ouija board winks
before revealing alphabetical secrets

The Spark
By Stephen C. Curro

Katrina grew up in a frigid world ruled by a tyrant. By day, she works as a mechanic. At night, she becomes the Ace, the King's personal assassin. She's not proud of her job, but she's accepted that it's the way things are. At least she has her boyfriend Dez and his little brother Uriah to light her life.

When Katrina is ordered to quash a rebel attack on the King's Command Center, she thinks it's just another job. But as she uncovers the plot, she is shocked to learn that Dez may be involved with the dissidents. Now Katrina must make an impossible choose—eliminate the one she loves, or defy the King she swore to serve.

The Spark is a sci-fi thriller about love, betrayal, and how the futures of others, even a whole civilization, can be determined through a single choice.

https://www.hiraethsffh.com/product-page/the-spark-by-stephen-c-curro

planetary conformity
Lee Clark Zumpe

we softened the angry red face of Mars
by growing a beard of green;

we filled the craters of our lunar neighbor
with distilled water, creating giant swimming pools.

we scattered the greenhouse clouds of Venus,
now we can ski the slopes of Sapas Mons.

we punched Jupiter right in its big red eye,
stopped winds once clocked at 900 miles per hour.

we took a break in exclusive retreats and posh resorts
scattered across the rings of Saturn.

drunkenly, we broke the ice on Pluto
and turned Uranus into a cozy shopping mall.

now that the terraformers have packed up their gear,
and headed over to Neptune for a beer,

we can rest assured that no matter where we go,
we'll always be here.

Onboard The U.S.S. Somoza
Alan Ira Gordon

Meet me in a country in the Third World.
The text screen fluttered like an aged moth beating out its last breath.

Perhaps it was the ocean breeze affecting the half-expected message. Or maybe my hand trembled with anger, flamed by the intrusion of Aaron into yet another vacation. It really didn't matter. The message was here, as it had arrived so many times before, always delivered when I was alone on the beach.

Aaron Nakasone would give me a few days to unwind, snuffle amidst the string bikinis, assimilate a coating of suntan oil, salt and sand, let my heart fill anew. Then he would send the same text. Nakasone Baseball Scouting Bureau LLC had a tip, a sure thing. The single sentence's meaning was clear and precise.

Aaron wanted me onboard the *Somoza.*

Nothing's worse when visiting the Caribbean than arrival on Saint Thomas in the U.S. Virgin Islands. I cut through the reeking airport terminal toward the cabstands without bothering to check for my missing luggage and hailed a waiting Rasta driver.

"One for Bluebeard's Castle."

"For certain, Mon."

The van snaked amongst the island's hills, following cracked narrow bands of twisted concrete through greenery into the town of Charlotte Amalie. The van deposited me at the white stucco walls and red-tiled roof of Bluebeard's Castle Hotel.

"Welcome home, Mr. Jones," said the front desk clerk.

"Good to be back, Ralphie. Although you know that I'm not really at home, out here."

"Ah, but home is where the heart is," he laughed. "And your heart must be in our hills, for you do return time and again."

"My heart is in the beaches," I replied as I signed in.

"Are you still scouting for the Nippon Ladies League?"

"Yeah, Nakasone's got me doing Tonto work for the Chiba City Pussycats this season."

"*Real men* do not watch ladies play baseball," Ralphie sniffed. "I do not understand why the Japanese are so entertained by women playing the game."

"You're a prince of equality, Ralphie."

Ralphie gestured toward a dreadlocked assistant. "Alfredo, Room 314 for my favorite guest, Mr. Bitterness Jones! May his stay on Saint Thomas be carefree!"

"It's all work, Ralphie, believe me. Chiba City needs speed on the basepaths this season and I'm here to find it."

"Then try the Myrmidons, Mon," Ralphie replied in a low voice. "They have a *bolt* of lightning by the name of Sukie LaMont this season."

"I'll check'er out, old friend."

'You let me know, Mon, you need any 'ting else."

I glanced at my watch and headed toward my room for a quick shower. Early evening would be a good time to get down to *The Cocoa Elephant* for my marching orders.

The Cocoa Elephant was crowded for a weekday evening.

I snagged a beer at the bar and headed for the back of the room as Fractal Jimmy And His Eisenhower Band ripped into their local island hit, "Play Nixon For Me." It was best for me to slouch low at a table in the rear. The last thing I needed was for Fractal to spot me this early in the scouting. If he knew I was here so soon to check-out one of his team's girls, things could get sticky.

I was halfway through my beer when a familiar voice rumbled-up from behind.

"*Bitter*, my lad, how unexpected a pleasure!"

A Bacon triplet eased his immense bulk down across from me.

"Which one are you?" I asked cautiously. "Rags, Tags or Obadiah?"

When the Senator died and left the Myrmidons to his asshole kid, his will specified that Fractal Jimmy had to keep the Bacon triplets on for team general management. Smart man, that Senator. I wouldn't trust the bastard with a ballteam, either.

My problem was that only one Bacon boy was in Aaron's pocket and I could never tell the three of them apart.

"I'm Obadiah, yuh damn Yankee."

I relaxed.

"How goes the season, Obie Wan?"

"We've got a good team, this year. A few chicks who could really tear-up the Jap league in a year or two."

Obadiah put his own beer up to his cherubic face. I watched half the bottle's contents slough-out in one easy motion. He burped.

"So tell me, Bitterness. Are you here to meet the Buddha-Man?"

"You know Aaron hasn't left Osaka in thirteen years. Why in hell I get those "meet me" messages, I'll never know. You always give me the lowdown, once I'm here."

"He still sends out the message, huh? Our Nakasone is a superstitious one."

We nursed our drinks in silence for awhile. Then I leaned in.

"There's a U.S. Navy missile frigate in the harbor, Obie."

"No shit. Toys that big are pretty tough to miss."

"There's also no sailors in the Elephant tonight. Which means no shore leave. What's going on?"

Obie glanced around the room. "Fractal used some pull with one of the Senator's old colleagues and got the ship down here. One of his security patrols around the *Somoza* thought they spotted a pack'a dolphins."

I burst-out laughing. "You have got to be fracking kidding!" I gasped. "The U.S. government's wasting taxpayer's defense dollars on a myth that only exists in your moron boss's mind!?"

"Look, Bitter, you and I know that Jimmy's nuts. But fact is, last season the Japs bought up thirty-five percent more minor league player contracts from our league here than from the Nicaraguan League. The big leaguers love to play the Caribbean minors against each other, keep us lean'n mean. Personally, I think a scout from the Jap league re-dredged up the attack dolphin rumor just to see how we'd handle it."

I could hardly get the words out, I was laughing so hard. "That's it...I admit it...Aaron sent me here with a pack of suicide bomber Flippers to sink the *Somoza*...we attack at dawn...the attack code is 'Tell'em Charley sent ya!'"

"You're a real comedian, Jones."

"You're right," I wheezed. "Still, I can't wait to hear the street talk on this one, next time I'm pulling Tonto work in Managua!"

Obadiah glanced nervously toward the empty stage. It was time to get down to brass tacks.

"So Obie, who does Aaron want me to check out?"

"I'll text you her file. Name's Sukie LaMont. We bought her contract from the Marlins and she's been picking-up speed every week. This babe's got enough talent to very well bust into the Jap all-star team in about two seasons."

"Why's Aaron so big on her?"

Obadiah shook his head. "All's I know is I texted a bunch of the new girl's files out to Aaron and he says to have you check-out Sukie LaMont and no one else when you pop-up."

I drained the last of my beer. "The Buddha-Man's been sucking down saki so long, he wouldn't know real talent if it bit him in his ass. You think she's got what it takes?"

"Well, I'm not really sure..." he drifted off, staring down at his fingernails.

"Ralphie at Bluebeard's thinks so."

Obadiah looked-up startled. "Ralphie has a big mouth."

"Ralphie knows his shit. Any other Tontos on to her, yet?"

"Nope. Rags and Tags have been keepin' her under wraps." Obadiah drummed his pudgy fingers on the table. "Fractal ordered'em not to promote her to anyone yet. He's pissed at her, put'er on suspension for a week."

"No kidding, what'd she do? Maybe I can talk the rest of the team into doing the same thing."

Obie laughed. "Don't you and the Fractal start in again!"

"So what's got Sweet Baby James in an uproar?"

Obadiah stood and wiped his hands on his shirt. "You come-on out to the *Somoza* tomorrow morning. I'll show you what put Sukie in the doghouse."

The next morning I snagged a skiff pilot in-port, who headed-out along the island's west coast toward the *Somoza*. Forty-five minutes into the trip and we spotted the U.S. missile frigate just outside Magens Bay. The *Somoza* was anchored beyond her at the mouth of the bay, basking like a giant whale in the morning sun.

The entire idea of the *Somoza* was armored proof that as the old song goes, paranoia runs deep.

She was originally British, an *Invincible Class* light aircraft carrier berthing Sea Harrier VTOL fighter jets. The Senator had picked her up for a song when the Brits began dismantling their navy and berthed her up in Long Beach, near the *QE II*. Back when Fractal Jimmy's rivalry with the Nicaraguans first flared, someone at *The Cocoa Elephant* joked about hiding the team from Nicaraguan Tonto surveillance out at sea. An idea was sparked in Jimmy's fried brain and the following season the craft was moved to Saint Thomas.

Tourists visiting the beach could see the ship hulked-out offshore, her deck expanded opposite the carrier's superstructure side to better duplicate the dimensions of a Nippon League ballfield.

My skiff docked alongside the *Somoza* under the glaring eye of a patrol boat loaded down with Navy SEALS. I clambered up aluminum steps to top deck, passed through a chain link fence and emerged onto emerald grass. Obadiah waddled toward me.

"What a morning! I forgot what it's like to be up here! Sorry I'm late, I took the scenic route to get here."

"Late? Like I'm supposed to give a flying fuck that you're back?"

"You're not Obie, are you?"

"I'm Rags, you moron. But I wouldn't expect a Tonto to have the brains to tell us apart."

Obie appeared from behind me. "Ignore his lousy sense of humor, Bitterness. He's just antsy because he hasn't got a friend in the world except for Tags. And that's not saying much."

The pair glared at each other a moment until Obie won a silent struggle with Rags stomping away, shaking his head and muttering.

"It's got nothing to do with you. C'mon."

The field deck was deserted, save for two players running sprints down aft. I followed Obadiah, dodging sprinklers rainbowing a mist of moisture across the grass, until we reached a maintenance lift touched against the edge. Obie ambled over to a control box.

"Hop on."

"What for? The stairs aren't good enough anymore to go below deck?"

"I'm lowering you shipside. You do want to see what Sukie LaMont did to piss-off Fractal, don't you?" He locked down the safety railing. "Relax, I'm only sending you down a bit. Just face shipside." He pulled a lever and the lift hummed downward.

Rusted sheet bolts rose upward as the platform glided down. Then it began, bright orange arcs of spray paint contrailing from my feet, forming letters as they came waist high, then words at eye level. The platform stopped with a chunking noise.

I stepped back as far as I could, ignoring the rail digging into my back.

Nine words.

Obie knew me too well.

I couldn't wait to meet Sukie LaMont.

The lift began to rise. When I reached topdeck Obie was standing with Sukie in tow. She was about a head under my height, with violet eyes and brunette hair pulled-back into a player's ponytail. It was her face that did it for me, intelligence and openness with a dash of kindness thrown in for good measure. This was a woman patient and smart enough to withhold judgment beyond a first impression.

Obie did the intros. "Bitterness Jones. Sukie LaMont, second base. Sukie, Bitter."

"How do you do, Bitter."

"Fine, Sukie, I'm pleased to meet you. I've heard good things."

Obie prattled-on about why I was here and the opportunity that Nakasone LLC could offer to Sukie.

"Jones should probably check out your speed for himself."

Sukie looked at me, measuring. "We could do that now."

"I prefer to do my scouting in my usual way. I'd like to meet you on the island tomorrow morning at Red Hook."

We all smiled and nodded as everything was set for tomorrow. A sudden thought occurred.

"By the way, Sukie."

"Yeah?"

I pointed toward the maintenance lift. "Obie sent me down. You do nice work."

She looked at me with a hint of smile. Then she nodded and turned away.

I was waiting dockside at Red Hook when Sukie hopped-out of a cab van on time. Her ponytail was topped by a lime green baseball cap, letter "M" in bold white.

We clambered onto a boat I'd chartered and settled into deck chairs aft as the charter captain fired-up the engines. Sukie gazed around the harbor.

"First time you've been down to Red Hook?"

"Yeah, I haven't had much time for sightseeing since the Myrmidons bought my contract."

"Who'd you play for before that?"

"I was in the Bayou League back home in N'Orleans. Started second base for the Crawmamas."

The pieces suddenly fell into place. Speed on the basepaths and Obie's protective patronage. "You're Adrian LaMont's daughter, aren't you?"

Sukie eyed me warily. "That's one way of putting it. I never forgave her for her years with the Osaka Tigresses. Me and my daddy saw her maybe three times back then. MVP awards don't tuck a little girl into bed at night." She waited on my reply.

I really didn't want to reply. Adrian LaMont's abandoning her family while her celebrity raged in Japan was a brutal legend of the game. But I had to ask the obvious question. "But you're following in Adrian's footsteps."

"I really haven't decided yet if the game is worth it. Given what happened to Adrian and all."

Our boat eased out of the harbor. The trip between The Two Saints takes about an hour on a calm day and it wasn't long before we dropped anchor at Honeymoon Beach over at St. Johns. The captain launched a dingy and we were quickly on the beach.

Sukie began her loosening routine. "Nice place for a scouting test," she said, rotating her neck.

"It is a nice stretch of sand, although I've seen a few better."

Sukie moved into a stretch-and-bend routine. "A few better, huh? Obie said you're a fanatical beach-goer. A real New Englander. A damn Yankee."

"Thanks a lot."

"It's not a compliment, it's an accusation!" I laughed.

"I have but one defense. As my damn Yankee ancestors would say, 'And all the people shouted, from Nahant to Olde Cape Cod, of a truth our Noble Daniel is a Down-East God."

Sukie continued her routine. "That's not half-bad. Where'd you hear that?"

"You like it? I found it in an old newspaper back in Massachusetts when I was a sports reporter, before I got into scouting."

"Do you still write stuff to keep from rusting?"

"No, I don't."

"Why not?"

"I'll tell you why. See those rocks down the beach? There's a metal bar in the sand just before them. From here to the bar and back is the length around a Nippon League stadium basepath."

I held my right arm over my head, the stopwatch glistening. "Let's see what the daughter of Adrian LaMont can do." The stopwatch clicked.

She was off like a shot, legs tense like steel pistons, kicking-up tufts of hard sand with her heels. She got off on an excellent low kick, reached the rocks, tapped the bar and reversed. I silently counted.

Too soon she passed me in a blur. As she trotted back I looked at the stopwatch. Shook it once. Then twice. Looked at it again. Shook it some more. Kept on looking.

Sukie stood next to me, hands on her knees and breathing deeply. "How much did I break the old Honeymoon Beach record by?"

"A lot." I paused. "Tell me, Sukie. Do you want to play for Chiba City?"

"I suppose any of the girls back on the *Somoza* would jump at the chance. But like I said before, I'm not sure if the game is for me. I think that's why I graffitied the ship. I was kind of hoping that the decision would be made for me.

"Tell me, Bitter, you still haven't answered my question. Why'd you stop writing sports?"

"It just didn't mean much to me. It was like being a human tape recorder of games."

"It couldn't have been that mundane. You must have felt some creativity."

I took a step toward Sukie. "I haven't seen anything creatively written in awhile. Until yesterday. Spraypainted on the side of that big tin bucket."

Sukie didn't hesitate at all, leaning forward and kissing me, moving into my arms. We stayed like that for a long time until I was aware of the sound of the boat's engines coughing to life. We gathered-up our stuff and got back to the boat. Sitting aft on the trip back, I took her hand in mine. "What now, Sukie?"

Her violet eyes washed over my face. "Now we go back to Bolongo Bay."

We fell into it all really hard, settling into her Bolongo Bay beach bungalow. I had Ralphie send Alfredo down with my stuff and told him not to tell Aaron where I was.

Minutes. Hours. Day and night. The next week just flowed as one. She went out alone to the *Somoza* once. I couldn't stand the day without her and went along each time thereafter. Sometimes Obie would come top deck with old-school message print-outs from Aaron. I would fold them into paper airplanes and launch them over the side at patrolling Navy SEALS.

"Why does Fractal Jimmy hate you?" Sukie asked one night.

I laughed. "You mean to say you never heard the story at *The Cocoa Elephant*?"

"Nope."

"It's a little weird. We never got along, but the final straw wasn't intentional on my part, although Fractal will never believe it. Do you know who Anastasio Somoza was?"

"Wasn't he some dictator in Nicaragua before democracy?"

"Uh-huh. So when the Senator docked the *Somoza* at Long Beach it still had some stuffy British name. When Fractal hauls'er down to Magens he replaces the name, rechristens her as...get this...the *U.S.S. Jack Nicholson*."

Sukie laughed as I continued. "It was classic Fractal. The name's painted-on and Jimmy holds a wild christening ceremony, the talk of the island. Not long after, the first Nicaraguan suicide bomber dolphin rumor starts floating around. In the Elephant one night I made a harmless joke about it, saying something like, 'it's not even worth worrying about, it's not as if Jimmy offended the Nicaraguan League by naming the tub after Somoza."

"Where's the punchline?"

"I know, it's real flat. The thing is, people were scared, actually believed that the rival league would send attack dolphins to hit the ship. The room explodes with tension-breaking laughter and everyone's buying me drinks. Within the week, everyone in Town's calling the tub the *Somoza*. Jimmy goes ape-shit and in his loony logic has the *Nicholson* logo painted over, like in his anger he's punishing the world."

"That's wild! Aren't you worried he'll do something for revenge?"

"Not really. He needs Nakasone Scouting to keep him ahead of the Nicaraguans and Cubans with the Nippon big leagues, so we just stay out of each other's way. Besides, I guess we can call it even. Jimmy's the one who stuck me with the nickname "Bitterness" not long after. Claimed I was a bitter New England Puritan, with a sense of humor to match."

"Some Puritan. I want the real first name Jones, now!" She shrieked as I tickled her ribs then she counterattacked with a vengeance, breaking all defenses with her kisses. "You'll have to tell me tomorrow night, anyway. You'll spill it as an anniversary present."

"Anniversary?"

She poked at my side. "Yes! Anniversary! It's one week ago tomorrow that we went over to Honeymoon Beach! I expect wining and dining!" She hit me with a pillow. "Tomorrow night, I draw the Mason-Dixon line! I expect the elusive truth to be revealed!"

"How about dinner and then a moonlit trip to Honeymoon Beach?"

She paused in her pillowing and blew a stray lock of hair from her face. "Agreed." She pounced anew, shouting "The South will rise again!"

I borrowed a cruiser and we made the crossing under a full moon. I eased the boat off the beach and dropped anchor, the moon bathing the familiar sandy stretch with an opaque glow. We settled-in ashore on a blanket and I gave her my one-week anniversary present, a silver chain and pendant with a Larimar stone center, the Caribbean turquoise mineral shining in the sandy glow. Sukie fingered the stone.

"One more present, Bitter. The name."

"Right, the name." I reached into my pocket and produced the stopwatch. "If you beat your old time you get the name. Should be no problem, right?"

"Jonesy, you worm!" She laughed and tossed sand at me. "The name, now!" We rolled around laughing and coughing with sand. After awhile she stood up and stared down at me defiantly, fists on her hips. "Fine, you're on!"

I stood and raised the stopwatch over my head and clicked.

She was off, a blur in the moonlight. I watched and steadily counted, squinting as she reached the metal bar, tapped it and reversed. Five yards. Ten. Fifteen.

Sukie glanced toward the water and straightened forward. Then did a hard double-take. She stumbled to her hands and knees and stayed down, staring into the water. Then she turned and scampered crab-like away from the water, crying-out.

"Sukie!"

I ran down the beach and dropped to my knees beside her.

"In...the water...don't..." she coughed.

I turned on my knees toward the water. Something big was silently bobbing in place not too far offshore. I stood and walked into the wash.

Fractal's dolphin nightmare lived. Correction. This one didn't.

This looked to be a small-sized Flipper before its tail was sheared away. I tried not to look at the damage as I focused on a wide golden band encircling its midpoint. It was armor, a fine mesh of squares girthing the beast like a golden truss. I bent and pressed my palms firmly on each side of the carcass to guide it landward. The form rippled slowly through the shallow water.

A sudden urge seized me. I headed down the beach to the dingy and paddled-out to the boat. Rummaging a bin I found a tarp, brandy bottle and a shovel. I paddled backshore and hauled the stuff down the beach.

I gently sat Sukie in the dingy and wrapped our blanket around her shoulders. She was shaking, staring aimlessly out to sea. I put the brandy bottle to her lips and tilted. She swallowed, then sputtered a line of liquor down her chin. I poured more into a cup for her then grabbed the tarp and dragged it oceanward.

The dolphin was mired at the shoreline. I went to work. The sucker was like a lead weight on dry land. Time passed as I rolled and prodded the beast inland, inches at a time. Sweat stung my eyes and my arms and legs screamed for rest as we made our way up the beach. Eventually, we were at a point where it felt right.

I retrieved the shovel and dug.

Dawn filtered into the shallow trench. Using the shovel as a lever, I rolled the dolphin in and covered it with the tarp, then finished filling-in the grave. I jabbed the shovel into the sand and walked over to Sukie.

She was looking seaward. "It was heading for the *Somoza*."

"We should tell them."

Sukie turned toward the grave. "No," she said firmly. "Let a storm toss it up for a ranger to find. If the navy can't stop'em then the ship deserves it."

"But-"

"No. This isn't our game."

She stood and wrapped her arms around me. "Take me to Chiba City," she said.

The half-life of catharsis can seem eternal, even if the calendar says it's only been days. We stayed at Bolongo Bay for a time as the edges of it began to dull over. The light began to rise again in Sukie's eyes.

I played the Tonto game well after that. Sent a few messages of my own to Aaron, enrolled Obie in the cause and wheeled and dealed my way into a Chiba City contract for Sukie.

We took a last ride out to the *Somoza* for Sukie to pick up her stuff. As she headed for the superstructure I wandered the green field and soon found myself at the maintenance lift. I stepped onto the lift and locked-in the safety railing. Rusted bolts rose until the platform silently stilled.

They were taking their own tropical time removing it, the letters fading from the ongoing effort. But it was still legible. I re-read from left to right, the short poetic line which first hinted of my soulmate.

The Heart Has Reasons Which Reason Does Not Understand.

Too soon the platform began to rise. Sukie stood by the controls, tears streaking her cheeks. "I'm not going to Chiba City. I won't be a part of it anymore! Animals turned into hell machines over a damned game! If I stay in it, I'll lose myself and end up like my Momma!"

"Jason."

"Huh?" She looked up, sniffling.

"My first name is Jason. Like in *The Argonauts*."

Sukie stared at me. Then laughed. "You don't need a golden fleece. You've found me."

I looked at her. "That's incredibly pathetic."

Sukie took her baseball cap off her head and whacked me with it, then flung it outward. It tumbled slowly downward, one shot in a thousand, alighting on the bow of a SEAL patrol boat. A crewman grabbed it, looked up and waved, then put it on backwards as the patrol rounded the *Somoza's* bow and slipped out of sight.

I learned two things from my last scouting of the *Somoza*.

One is that man has an innate and natural talent to bring even the most ludicrous of nightmares into this world. The other is that love can balance the equation, even the scales and somehow make it all livable.

One lesson bitter.

One lesson sweet.

We've lived here in Santa Monica for a number of years, now. I teach creative writing at the local community college, while Sukie coaches the college women's baseball team.

The Nicaraguans finally hit the *Somoza* sometime after we left. The internet showed the big hull listing like a bobbing dolphin, Navy patrols scrambling like angry water bees. It wasn't a fatal shot but it did hit the mark enough for Fractal Jimmy's paranoia to finally take him over the edge. He sold the team to a Norwegian sardine exporter who abandoned the ship for a normal island-side ballpark.

Sukie and I still talk about the dolphin sometimes. Our youngest girl Rebecca is too young to listen, but sometimes her big sister Adrian will pull herself up into my lap and follow the conversation. "Bad dolphin, Daddy?" she once asked, her large violet eyes looking up wonderingly.

"No, honey," I answered. "good dolphin." Only bad people, I thought to myself as she snuggled into my arms. We've made it a point to take the girls to Sea World occasionally and familiarize them with some well-treated and happy Flippers.

I'm still a beach person, although I now feel best on sand crowded with humanity. I don't need the beach to make my heart fill anymore, though. Whether we're on the sand with the girls or off somewhere else, a day doesn't go by that I don't make a point to tell her.

I love you so much, Sukie.
Each day begins with you.

Tales From the Quantum Café by Alan Ira Gordon

A collection of oddments created over lunch—you'll find them in this volume. There's an homage to the Thimble Theater; a treatment of the Revolutionary War in terms of a baseball game; small-town environmental problems; a random pun here and there; life on the Outback; the secret of the Drake equation; an off-beat look at Disney; and much, much more!

https://www.hiraethsffh.com/product-page/tales-from-the-quantum-cafe-by-alan-ira-gordon

The Future Adventures of
Bailey Belvedere

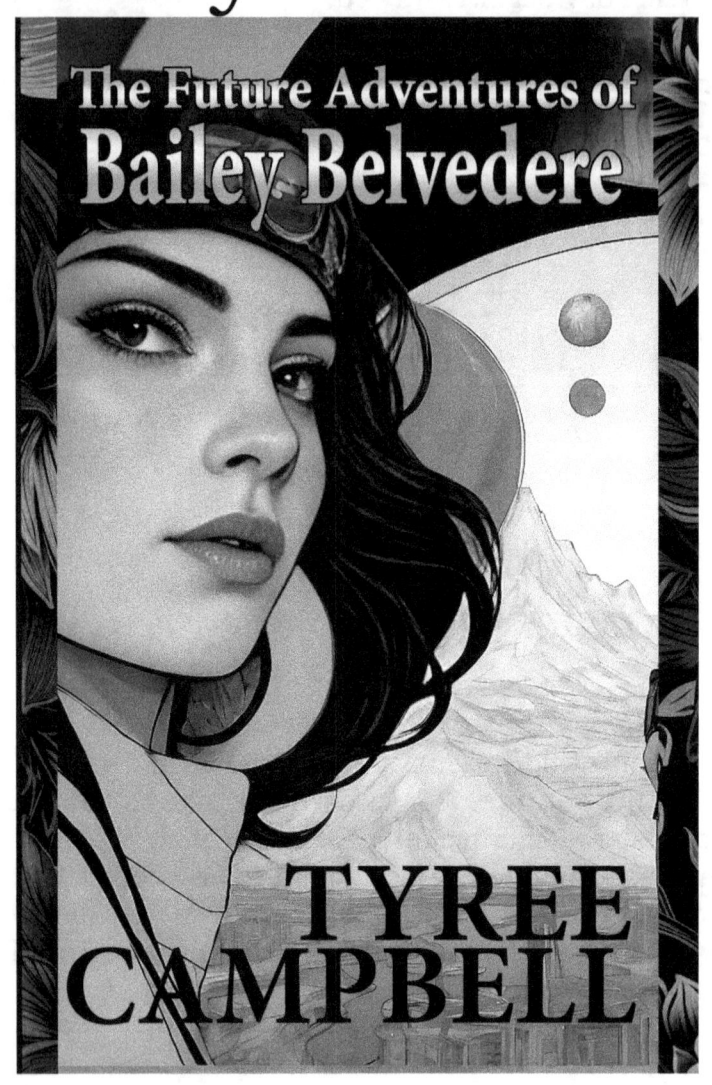

As the societies of Earth collapse into chaos and destruction, Bailey Belvedere, a U.S. Army Intelligence officer fighting for her very survival, steals aboard an alien spacecraft, and soon finds herself given the authority and power by a superior alien entity to intervene in various problems in the Galaxy. Along the way she frees a world from interstellar slave traffickers, deals with an AI who becomes pregnant, inadvertently destroys a waffle house, fights against the abductors of a special child, and generally finds herself in some sort of trouble from one moment to the next.

Type: Novel – science fiction

Ordering Links:

Print Edition: https://www.hiraethsffh.com/product-page/further-adventures-of-bailey-belvedere-by-tyree-campbell

PDF Edition: https://www.hiraethsffh.com/product-page/further-adventures-of-bailey-belvedere-by-tyree-campbell-1

Listening To Dandelions
George Anthony Kulz

Frail hands hold the stem
Teaming with white seeds
Gossamer travelers ready to take flight
A wish, a teardrop, a shaky breath
And white puffs release
Parachute away
Light carriers of heavy loads

On a spring wind
Impossible dreams make their way
To improbable places
Through cracks in walls
And splits in fallen logs
And beyond the border
Between the living and the dead

Spring turns to summer
And summer to fall
The seasons as transient
As those tiny seedlings
Taking root along the way
Planting their messages
In hearts long gone to earth

Fall is the season
Dead hearts beat again
If only for a short time
They long for life
The arms of loved ones
The warmth of a touch
Reminders of days long past

One long-lost lover
Hearing whispered promises
Messages carried by dandelions
Taking seed in the ground

Rises from his deep slumber
And follows backwards
Through the dandelions' time

To the source
To a residence
To the living

To her

The Oculist's Daughter
By Angel Favazza

The Oculist's Daughter by Angel Favazza is a steampunker in the old west. It's got a semi-mad scientist (her dad), her, of course, plus outlaws, Indians, Wyoming, a poison gas for killing natives, and an Indian guide. It all adds up to a rollicking adventure.

https://www.hiraethsffh.com/product-page/oculist-s-daughter-by-angel-favazza

Sky Shrieks
David Castlewitz

The third anniversary of Carsin's sister's death would be as difficult as the first two. No one said it, but Carsin knew what everyone thought. He could've saved Alia, but chose not to. Now, while he walked alongside Walan Creek, the site of the skirmish where Alia died, Carsin looked for a pebble for his sister's memorial mound. It didn't need to be a valuable stone.

In the distance, the fluttering flags and pennants of the Wingless – he thought of the dominant species in vulgar and derogatory terms – marked where a merchant caravan had camped at the edge of Skaylor territory.

Overhead, a trio of Skaylors glided on the wind, keeping tabs on the intruders. According to the news in the village, the merchants wanted to negotiate payment so they could pass through the valley, but Wingless often used that ruse before attacking to force their way through.

Another squadron of six leapt from a high cliff, their wings positioned for maximum lift. They rose in arrow formation before executing a rapid descent that made the bone-carved whistles at the tips of their leathery wings shriek.

Carsin meandered alongside the creek, a stone for his sister's memorial in his hand. His medic-rescue squad-mates lazed on the grassy slopes bordering the gurgling waterway. Carsin didn't think there'd be a need to rescue anyone. There'd be no fighting today. These merchants weren't like the treasure hunters who trespassed in the valley, or the trophy seekers looking to kill a Skaylor for sport. They just wanted to take the easiest route through the mountains to the coastal plain to sell their wares.

Watching the airborne Skaylors gave Carsin a twinge of jealousy. His stunted wings, a condition that afflicted one of every five of his kind, kept him grounded. Like his medic-rescue teammates. But he doubted that any of them had a famous dead sister and a disparaging father to remind him of his physical fault.

Might as well get on with the mental whipping, Carsin thought when the duty day ended and the rescue team melted away from the mountain slope. Might as well give the old man a chance to vent in private, before friends and other family gathered for Alia's commemoration.

He walked with his head down, his pointed beak nearly touching his chest, his feet knowing the well-used path to the family homestead. When he reached its outskirts, he looked up to see his father standing on the porch, his scarred hands on the railing, his wings quivering beneath his knee-length shirt.

"You're early," Father rasped.

"In case you need help," Carsin said.

"I hired some younguns."

Carsin stood at the porch steps. He and his older sister used to jump from the top of the porch to practice the leaps they'd make as adults. But his wings never matured. They remained flabby chunks of leather sticking to a thin webbed structure of bone and sinew. He couldn't glide on the wind.

"Negotiations with the merchants went well today," Carsin said.

"You didn't have anything to do with it."

"My unit was the rescue team in case – "

"Don't make yourself sound important. I didn't like it when you were a kid and I don't like it now. Your sister never bragged about anything. She just did her job. She'd still be with us if you'd done yours."

Carsin fingered the stone in his pocket. He looked at his pointed shoes and at the way his baggy pants fell at his ankles in a heap of coarse cloth. At the sound of a door hinge's squeak, he raised his eyes to watch his father go into the house. He didn't follow. He knew he wasn't welcome. He hadn't entered the sprawling home in three years.

The youngsters on the lawn set up tables, covered them with linen cloth, hustled dried meats and salted vegetables from the kitchen at the back of the house to three-legged stands spread across the front yard. Pitchers of wine and water were set out, along with tin cups emblazoned with the family crest: two fighters floating in the sky, wings spread.

Carsin meandered to the memorial plot at the side of the house. A large stone marked the spot where his sister's bones were interred in a wooden ossuary. The tribute mound, made of pebbles contributed by her mourners over the past three years, had grown only a little in height. Many of the stones had fallen to one side of the fragile tower.

At the sound of his name, he looked sideways, and smiled at his younger sister, Janely. Eyes wide, she seemed to float across the short distance separating them, her small mouth parted in a grin, her beak not yet pointed, not yet at its adult length and shape.

"I always think you won't show," she said.

"Did you hear from Mother?"

A sad look came into Janely's large gray eyes. Their mother had abandoned the family after Alia's death. She went north to the Grand Temple and joined a monastery.

Other guests swarmed the front lawn as the sun fell. They drank, sat at the tables and ate, stood in small groups and talked, and settled down on the grass in front of Alia's memorial plot to tell stories about her.

Carsin drifted in that direction. He hoped no one would ask him to speak. They hadn't in previous years. What would he say? Tell them about her final moments when she barged ahead to hold off a band of treasure hunters who'd raided the valley. Carsin had carried several wounded to an aid station at the mountain wall. The most severely wounded would be put on cable cars and taken through a tunnel to the plateau above. That was standard procedure. Carsin, though lightly armed, wasn't expected to jump into a melee and fight.

Alia did that quite well. She and her Second, a massively built female named Fanzee often fought side-by-side, firing off the four rounds in their handguns and then resorting to using their short swords. They were heralded as powerful warriors who inspired others. No one expected they'd ever lose a fight. They'd certainly never lose when they fought together.

"I'll put my stone down now."

Startled, Carsin shivered at the sound of Fanzee's husky voice. She brushed by him and a warm glow filled his skinny neck, his narrow face flushing.

Fanzee dropped to her knees, her dress spilling out behind her, covering her wide rump. She usually wore a one-piece uniform, a tight-fitting garment that bared her back and showed off her muscles and strong legs. She set a pale yellow pebble on top of the mound and mouthed a prayer to Deera, the goddess of wind, the deity Carsin's mother now served at the monastery.

"I'll pay my respects to Lord Pens," Fanzee said, nodding in the direction of Carsin's father.

"Don't remind him of how important he is," Carsin quipped.

Fanzee laughed, her peak dipping up and down, reddening at the tip. "You two are at it again."

"Why wouldn't we be?" Carsin countered. "He doesn't know what happened at the creek."

Fanzee strode across the lawn to where Carsin's father stood surrounded by his admirers, all of them commiserating with him about his lost, as though it had happened only yesterday.

Janely strolled into view, a chubby male at her side. They kept their heads close together, cheeks touching. When she drew close, she introduced her friend as Kitter.

"Kitter's composing an epic poem about our sister," Janely said.

Carsin coughed to hide his amusement. "About Alia?" As he spoke, their father stepped towards them, a cup of wine in his hand. Some splashed over the rim and he quickly took a gulp.

"Kitter?" Pens said. "Janely's told me about you."

The poet bowed his head, his oversized shirt billowing out at his belly.

Carsin cringed when his father turned towards him. He waited for a verbal slap, but his father showed only disgust before moving on to join other guests and other conversations.

"I hope I can get some input from you," Kitter said.

"What sort of input?" Carsin asked.

"You're on a medic team, right?"

"Rescue service. I'm not a medic."

"I'd like to shadow you sometime."

"You'll get in the way."

"I'll try not to. If I spent some time with you I'd know more about what the fighters think and feel. It's research."

"Why don't you go in with the fighters then?"

"I can't glide. I'm a stub."

Carsin snorted. Stub. He didn't like that term. He glanced at Janely. The anger in her eyes didn't bother him. Let her be angry. He had no reason to be this chubby poet's friend.

"Think we can set something up?" Kitter asked.

"Do it," Janely urged. "It's for our sister."

You think Father's going to like this poet enough to give you his blessing? Carsin said to himself. He'll want you to pick a fighter as a consort.

"Do I have your cooperation?" Kitter asked.

Carsin looked the poet up and down, from his wide face to his knobby bare knees below the hem of his shirt.

"Just do it," Janely urged.

"Take him on a mission yourself," Carsin said.

"I can't glide," Kitter said. "I told you. I'm like you."

Carsin snorted and walked away.

***

Carsin inspected the rescue sleds. He checked they were secured to the cable, felt the greased front runners, and double checked that the straps used to lock in the injured weren't frayed at the edges or so stiff that they'd crack. Once he completed his careful once-over of all twelve sleds, he signaled, Thumbs-up.

Stepping back from the line of sleds spread out one after the other on the narrow plateau, he watched them file into the tunnel entrance like automatons at a fair, their runners grinding against the coarse soil. The pulley attached to the cable squeaked and moaned, the braided straps building up heat. Kids doused the straps with water all along the way.

Prisoners from past battles comprised a gang turning a wheel at the base of the mountain, providing motive power for the cable.. Herding them to work, bellowing at them and striking them when they faltered on the wheel was not a job that Carsin relished, though he had to serve at the prison camp one day out of every three hundred. Whenever he did, his father always found out and praised him. It was praise he didn't want to hear. There was nothing worthy about beating down the already beaten.

How many prisoners would today's action provide? Carsin wondered. A large force of treasure seekers had been spotted by the morning patrol. Maybe they'd come to free their comrades now turning the wheel. Perhaps they sought to capture a Skaylor for some ritual in their city. They – the Wingless from the lands beyond the mountains – regularly attacked for no good reason.

Rocky peaks rose all around, along with flat plateaus where Skaylor fighters assembled. They were too far off for Carsin to discern faces. He couldn't pick out his sister. He'd looked for her earlier in the vanguard massing near the line of sleds, but hadn't seen her. Perhaps she huddled in a shallow cave as part of the reserves. Or she could've been one of those on the morning patrol. Wherever she served, Carsin knew she was out there. Hopefully, he wouldn't find her wounded and dying.

"She's in the second wave."

Carsin turned to face Fanzee. In uniform she blended in with the other fighters who'd soon leap. A leather helmet covered her red-and-gold curls. Not even a trace of hair escaped out the back or down the sides. Her tightly fitted one-piece bodysuit bulged at her upper arms and thick calves. Her wings protruded from slits at her sides, below her shoulders.

"You're wondering where Janely is, aren't you?" Fanzee said. She smiled. "I've got something I need you to do."

Carsin looked past Fanzee and saw Kitter, outfitted in a white one-piece suit like Carsin's and every other medic-rescue team member, but with a blue brimless hat, not a red one, so he wouldn't be mistaken for someone who knew what to do in an emergency.

"No," Carsin said, realizing what Fanzee would ask, angry that she wouldn't let things rest. If Kitter composed a tribute to Alia, Father would have one more reason to boast about his favorite child.

"It'll be good for you, too," Fanzee insisted, as if she'd read Carsin's mind.

"Why don't you do it? Wait. I know why. Because you've got more important things to worry about. You've got your own reputation to burnish. You've got – "

"Just do it! Help him out. When was the last time I asked for a favor?"

Carsin looked up at a three-Skaylor squad floating overhead.

"Never," Fanzee said. "Now I'm asking. I want this for Alia. She was your sister, but she was also my friend, and I want this tribute written. I want to hear it recited. I want it done."

"I understand," he said, "but he better not get in the way." He glared at Kitter standing several yards off, hands at his back, a smile on his soft round face. He'd help him, but he didn't intend to let the poet enjoy the experience.

Kitter ambled over.

"Don't get in my way," Carsin said.

"I'll just watch. I won't even ask questions."

Carsin concentrated on his work. This was one time when he wished he'd been assigned to a rescue squad at the base of the mountain.

"Those flags," Kitter began, pointing at the fluttering pennants on a lower and more distant plateau.

Carsin shot him a look of "won't ask any questions?" And then explained. "Semaphores. To signal for another wave of fighters."

"I want to see what's going on down there."

Carsin gestured towards the cliff's edge. The only barrier to keep anyone from falling off was a safety rope enclosing a spot for commanders inspecting the action. Sometimes someone from the Council of Twelve would watch a battle from there.

In the valley, tiny dark figures moved from one rock outcropping to another. Those were the Wingless. Carsin sneered at how they fought. They didn't maintain formation. Every fighter for himself. No discipline. The Skaylors, on the other hand, dove straight down at the dark figures, the whistles at the ends of their wings screeching, the pistols in their hand firing off a full load of four rounds the moment they landed. Wherever Skaylors set down, the enemy took cover

Squad after squad hit the intruders. On landing, and after emptying their pistols, they waded in with swords swinging. Then they raced to the nearest tunnel, where they climbed the stairs, taking two or three stone-carved steps at a time. Up top, out on the plateau again, they took a dose of water before lining up to leap again.

From his vantage point, Carsin watched the wounded Skaylors pulled to safety and strapped to the rescue sleds. Vibrations ran through the bottoms of his feet when the cable started moving, taking the wounded into the tunnel and up inside the mountain.

Carsin rushed into action. Along with two other squad-mates, he helped the wounded to the aid station across a bridge spanning a crevice between adjacent plateaus.

Kitter watched, eyes wide, face beaming.

"Want to really see something?" Carsin asked after the last of seven fighters had been carried across the bridge. He stepped into the tunnel entrance and dropped down to a landing beneath the sleds' ramp. Kitter followed. He slipped on a puddle of blood, the heels of his hard leather shoes caught in the cuffs of his one-piece suit's pants legs. He complained about the dark.

Grinning, Carsin looked into the deep well beneath them. The staircase descended in a spiral, but the sledding ramp dropped at a steep angle. Kitter walked with both hands on the railings, each step taken carefully and slowly. Carsin easily outpaced him, left him far behind. At the next landing, a lone sentry offered a nod of recognition, a lighted candle with a reflector attached to the top of his helmet.

"Want a lamp?" the sentry asked. He didn't look happy being on guard duty instead of soaring on the wind.

"What's the fighting like?" Carsin asked, shaking off the offer of something to light his way. He could see well enough in the dim light filtering in from above and below, as well as the flickering candlelight from the sentries at each landing. Kitter, he imagined, struggled in the dark Good. Let him struggle.

"Tapered off," the sentry said. "Last messenger came up this way just a few minutes ago."

"Treasure hunters," Carsin said. "They never last long in a fight."

Kitter wheezed with the effort to speak. "They ever get to the tunnels?"

The sentry snorted and shook his head. Carsin motioned to Kitter to follow. Might as well take him all the way down. Give him a better taste of what he wanted.

"Are you armed?" Kitter asked, his voice wavering.

"Yeah. Sure." Carsin tapped the short sword strapped to his hip. It wasn't much of a weapon, but the poet hadn't asked how well he was armed.

The base of the tunnel widened. The ramp leveled off to an easy incline. The last flight of stairs plunged straight down at an acute angle. Carsin barreled ahead, leaving Kitter to pick his way down the metal steps.

"Stay back," Carsin hissed, stopping with one hand raised. He didn't like what he saw. Rather, what he didn't see. He hadn't planned on there being trouble. He expected to see guards lounging at the tunnel entrance. Two or three red-clad rescue workers should be waiting, alert and on edge. Instead, he saw them lying face down inside the tunnel while the clash of metal on metal filled the air outside.

"What's wrong?" Kitter asked.

"I told you to stay back." Carsin felt the poet's hot breath on the back of his neck If anything happened.... It would be Kitter's own fault. There'd be no blaming anyone. No one could point a finger at him, at least not in the same way they pointed at him when discussing his older sister's death.

Fanzee wouldn't like what happened, though. Janely would be angry and sad – both at the same time. But neither could blame him. Kitter wanted the experience of the battle, the feel of the danger, the allure of the fight. That's what he wanted to write about when he composed his epic to Alia.

"You wanted to know if they ever get into the tunnels? Well, they do. They'll be in this one in another minute."

Kitter went pale. It showed even in this dim light. His eyes bulged. His fingers twitched and his knees shook. Carsin grinned. Serves him right.

"Stay there and fight 'em off if you want," Carsin said, pushing his way past Kitter and springing up the stairway. He stopped halfway to the next landing. Some messenger must've brought word of the breach to the upper levels because a contingent of a dozen guards, all armed with pikes and swords as well as pistols, crowded the landing in phalanx formation.

"Hey, you," the guard commander yelled at Kitter. "Back up this way."

Kitter didn't budge. The fighting had moved to just inside the tunnel entrance. Three Skaylors dueled with a mob. Sword against sword. Fists thrown. Carsin guessed the treasure hunters had maneuvered in the dried-up riverbed or hid in the bushes, massing for this assault.

Now was the time for Kitter to run.

"That fool's going to get killed," the guard commander said. "Is he with you?"

Carsin enjoyed the imagined sight of Janely weeping for her friend. And Fanzee? Carsin didn't care,. Even if she guessed what had happened, how he left Kitter to fend for himself, she couldn't actually blame him. It was her idea to send Kitter here.

Suddenly, he flashed on the skirmish where Alia fell wounded. Fanzee had stopped him from going back for his sister. She didn't put a hand on his arm, or plead with him to help her into the tunnel and the safety it offered. She merely stumbled, hand out to break her fall, trailing blood from a cut in her side, and he couldn't abandon her, even when he looked back at Alia and saw her on her knees.

Kitter stood frozen in place, trembling. You can save him if you want to, Carsin heard at the back of his mind, and then jumped from the landing, half sliding down the metal staircase. He tackled Kitter, locked one arm around his arm, and pulled hard. The heavyset poet was dead weight.

Someone came to their aid. Together, they dragged Kitter to the staircase. Reaching it, the poet gripped the cold metal railings and pulled himself upright, then scurried up the steps to the crowded landing above, where a phalanx of guards welcomed him with laughter. Their commander pointed Kitter to the next flight of stairs.

Carsin backed up one step at a time, his right hand on the pommel of his short-sword. The guardsman who'd helped him had joined the fight at the tunnel's mouth. Two more guards jumped from the landing, falling in a crouch, then rising to full height, and forming a skirmish line with practiced ease.

The reinforcements pushed the invading mob out of the tunnel before they really had a toehold. Outside, shots were fired. Metal weapons clashed.

Carsin caught up to Kitter halfway to the top. The poet coughed and gasped, down on one knee, head bent.

"You'll be okay," Carsin said.

"I couldn't move," Kitter said. He looked at Carsin with tears in his eyes.

"Get up. We'll get to the top and – "

"I wanted the experience. Guess I got it. Except Alia wouldn't have froze like that. Fanzee doesn't. You didn't. Janely never froze like I froze. What's wrong with me?"

Carsin shrugged. He wasn't prepared for that question, and he didn't want to say that he'd frozen a few times, too. "Next time, you won't freeze."

"There's not going to be a next time," Kitter said. "I've had enough."

Carsin helped Kitter stand.

"I don't think they appreciate what you do," Kitter said.

"You mean, my father?"

"Your little sister. Your father. Some others that I won't name. They don't appreciate the role you play. But don't worry. I'll set them straight. Alia won't be the only star in my epic."

Carsin watched Kitter's back recede from view, watched him step into the dim light at the end of the tunnel. He could've let him die back there, but he was glad he hadn't. Slowly, legs quivering from the adrenaline rush, Carsin climbed to the top of the stairs. At the final landing, he took the ladder up to the mouth of the tunnel.

"You want to hear my side of the story?" he asked Kitter.

"I do."

"I'll tell you exactly what happened. I saved Fanzee."

"And your sister?"

He remembered looking back and watching Alia go under with six or seven enemies hacking at her. "The truth is," he said, drawing in a long draft of air, "she saved me. Fanzee, too."

That was fact, he admitted to himself, giving Alia her due. She'd covered Fanzee's retreat to the tunnel. She covered his own efforts to save a wounded fighter. Other wounded Skaylors no doubt were saved as well because Alia fought on, even when she fell to her knees. It was time to stop denying that truth.

A Century Divides Us
Lee Clark Zumpe

Polarized by derivation,
we gaze through barbed wire fences;
a century divides us.

On one side is industry without dignity;
on the other, technology without conscience –
the decades are punctuated by inhumanities.

> Aboriginal faces, mud-caked and eager,
> mine shadows and harvest cities.
>
> Sterile faces, sedate and opaque and pale,
> encrypt divinities and forge sciences.

Different hands to build tomorrows,
different backs for different burdens,
different tongues to voice aspirations.

> A century divides us, there are no bridges.
> The cascade of history surges by beneath us.

Whispers from the Intoxicating Abyss
By Lee Clark Zumpe

You may not realize it, but they're out there: impossible shadows, omniscient horrors, and unseen, unknowable entities scattered across the great gulfs of nothingness at the edges of the universe. In this collection, author Lee Clark Zumpe draws back the curtain from the invisible realm, divulging its arcane secrets and ghastly revelations. Come walk paths meandering over shunned worlds adrift in darkness, and through seemingly mundane, liminal spaces that might be overrun with ancient shadows at any moment.

Stories are inspired by the works of H. P. Lovecraft.

Ordering links:
Print: https://www.hiraethsffh.com/product-page/whispers-from-the-intoxicating-abyss-by-lee-clark-zumpe

ePub: https://www.hiraethsffh.com/product-page/whispers-from-the-intoxicating-abyss-by-lee-clark-zumpe-2

PDF: https://www.hiraethsffh.com/product-page/whispers-from-the-intoxicating-abyss-by-lee-clark-zumpe-1

Speculative Fiction and Cultural Identity: Diverse Perspectives in the Genre
Yuliia Vereta

Speculative fiction, an expansive literary realm encompassing science fiction, fantasy, and horror, has emerged as a dynamic space where authors boldly explore cultural identity, diversity, and heritage. Within the vivid tapestry of speculative fiction, writers craft imaginative worlds and alternate realities that serve as powerful canvases for reflecting on their cultural roots, addressing pressing societal issues, and envisioning the future. This article delves into the myriad ways in which speculative fiction has evolved into a fertile ground for embracing and celebrating diverse perspectives on cultural identity.

Cultural Heritage as the Foundation of Worldbuilding
At the core of speculative fiction lies the remarkable art of worldbuilding. In this genre, authors often embark on the creative endeavor of constructing intricate and immersive settings that invite readers to journey into entirely different realms. It is within this process of worldbuilding that many writers draw upon their own cultural heritage to craft rich and authentic landscapes.

N.K. Jemisin, a prominent figure in contemporary speculative fiction, demonstrates the art of weaving cultural inspiration into worldbuilding in her celebrated "The Broken Earth" trilogy. In this masterwork, she seamlessly integrates elements from African, Caribbean, and African American cultures into a post-apocalyptic world. This intricate tapestry of cultural references imbues the story with a profound sense of authenticity. Jemisin's work not only tells a compelling narrative but also invites readers to explore diverse cultural perspectives within the confines of an engrossing fictional universe.

Similarly, Nnedi Okorafor, known for her captivating novels such as "Who Fears Death" and "Binti," draws upon her Nigerian heritage to infuse her narratives with the enchanting allure of African mythology and tradition. Okorafor's storytelling evokes the vibrancy and complexity of African culture while simultaneously engaging with contemporary societal issues.

Identity and Belonging: Navigating the Multifaceted Self
Speculative fiction frequently serves as a unique platform for probing questions of identity and belonging. Authors employ fantastical settings and enigmatic alien societies to dissect and understand the multifaceted experiences of marginalized communities and individuals. These narratives possess the extraordinary ability to deliver allegorical storytelling that resonates deeply with readers.

In Micaiah Johnson's thought-provoking novel "The Space Between Worlds," the protagonist possesses the extraordinary ability to traverse between parallel worlds, but with a critical caveat—she can only travel to those where her alternate selves have already met their demise. This tale is a profound exploration of privilege, identity, and intersectionality, as the protagonist navigates the intricate web of identities in a dystopian future. Johnson's work offers a commentary on the intricate nature of identity, emphasizing how cultural background and societal context are inextricably interwoven into our sense of self.

In "The City We Became" by N.K. Jemisin, New York City assumes a vibrant life of its own through the avatars representing its diverse boroughs. Each avatar embodies the unique cultural identities and histories of the city's neighborhoods. Jemisin's narrative celebrates the multiculturalism of the city while addressing the resilience of marginalized communities and confronting the challenges of gentrification and cultural erasure.

Resistance and Resilience in Alternate Realities: A Reflection of the Past and Present

Speculative fiction has also emerged as a vehicle for narratives of resistance and resilience in the face of cultural oppression and colonization. Authors skillfully employ the genre to explore the consequences of imperialism and the enduring struggle for cultural preservation.

In Ken Liu's poignant and heartrending collection of short stories, "The Paper Menagerie," the title story depicts a Chinese mother's extraordinary ability to breathe life into origami creatures through her magical paper-folding. This heartrending tale serves as a profound reflection on the immigrant experience and the relentless struggle to preserve cultural heritage in the face of assimilation. Liu's work stands as a poignant reminder of the importance of safeguarding cultural traditions and passing them on to future generations.

Sofia Samatar's remarkable novel, "A Stranger in Olondria," ventures into the heart of cultural imperialism and linguistic identity. The story follows Jevick, a young man from a remote island, on his journey to the continent of Olondria. Through his experiences, readers witness the tumultuous clash between native cultures and the relentless encroachment of colonial influence. Samatar's narrative underscores the remarkable power of language and storytelling in preserving cultural identity.

Intersectionality and Inclusivity: Celebrating Multifaceted Identities

The concept of intersectionality, which recognizes that individuals experience multiple forms of discrimination and privilege simultaneously, has become an essential cornerstone of discussions surrounding cultural identity. Speculative fiction readily embraces this notion by exploring the intricate intersections of cultural identity, race, gender, and sexuality.

In Naomi Alderman's thought-provoking novel, "The Power," a speculative element grants women the ability to generate electric shocks, fundamentally altering traditional power dynamics. The narrative engages with gender politics, but it also delves into how these dynamics intersect with race and other facets of identity. Alderman's work challenges readers to contemplate the complex and interwoven aspects of cultural identity and power.

Nalo Hopkinson's Caribbean-inspired science fiction novel, "Midnight Robber," delves deeply into issues of race, colonialism, and cultural heritage. Hopkinson's narrative explores the experiences of marginalized communities and underscores the significance of Afro-Caribbean traditions in shaping cultural identity. The novel serves as a powerful reminder of the importance of inclusivity and representation in the realm of speculative fiction.

A Multifaceted Kaleidoscope of Perspectives
In conclusion, speculative fiction has evolved into a multifaceted kaleidoscope of diverse perspectives on cultural identity. Through the remarkable technique of worldbuilding, authors have the power to capture and celebrate their cultural heritage, infusing their narratives with authenticity and depth. Through imaginative storytelling, they explore complex questions of identity, belonging, resistance, and intersectionality.

Speculative fiction has grown into a literary mirror that reflects the diverse tapestry of human experiences and cultural backgrounds. It invites readers to step into the lives of characters from various walks of life and provides a platform for underrepresented voices to be heard. As the genre continues to evolve, it remains a potent tool for fostering inclusivity, celebrating cultural diversity, and engaging with the complexities of identity in our ever-changing world.

Bibliography
1. Jemisin, N.K. "The Broken Earth Trilogy." Orbit, 2018.
2. Okorafor, Nnedi. "Who Fears Death." DAW Books, 2010.
3. Okorafor, Nnedi. "Binti." Tor.com, 2015.

4. Johnson, Micaiah. "The Space Between Worlds." Del Rey, 2020.
5. Jemisin, N.K. "The City We Became." Orbit, 2020.
6. Liu, Ken. "The Paper Menagerie." Saga Press, 2016.
7. Samatar, Sofia. "A Stranger in Olondria." Small Beer Press, 2013.
8. Alderman, Naomi. "The Power." Little, Brown and Company, 2016.
9. Hopkinson, Nalo. "Midnight Robber." Warner Books, 2000.

The Wolves of Glastonbury
by Edward Cox & Terrie Leigh Relf

What happens in Glastonbury stays in Glastonbury—even if it means the end of one of humanity's longest alternate lifelines. The hunt is on for Claire and Ethan . . .

https://www.hiraethsffh.com/product-page/wolves-of-glastonbury-by-terrie-leigh-relf-edward-cox

Helios
Zachary Grant

I miss the sun. It was the most under-appreciated star in the solar system. All anyone talked about was how it would kill us one day. Mom ranted about global warming all the time, but I've never understood the fuss. The sun getting hotter always sounded like good news to me, especially if it shone on my favourite spot.

Living in space isn't all bad. Some days are better than others. For example, today is a fantastic day. My morning starts when Mom's clock strikes five. The sunrise used to be my cue, but without it I've been learning to tell time. The five is my cue to wake her up. She loves it when I do that. She always grunts and waves her hand at me. I assume she's trying to pet me. I mean, who wouldn't. When she finally gets out of bed, I have to wait for her to make her coffee. She's so quiet before she drinks it, which is strange. Yelling gets me my food. It's the only way to get things done around here. I yell at her while she waits for her coffee to brew. Finally, breakfast is served.

Once she's all ready for the day, she kisses me on the head and leaves our tiny dorm. She tells me hers is the biggest on the station. Mom is a very important person. She deserves it.

All this sounds like a pretty standard morning. It doesn't become fantastic until I take the passage to my room. That's right, I've got my own place. Mom designed it to keep me entertained. For me to learn—get smarter. I want to be smarter, it's the only way I'll accomplish my secret mission. When I say secret, of course Mom knows. I tell her everything. That doesn't mean I need to tell the crew. She says it'll upset them, though I'm not sure why.

Mom knows how much I love the sun—how much I miss it. That's why my room has *artificial* sun. I'm not sure what that means, but it still feels good on my fur. I press the sun button with my paw, which showers the space in a beautiful glow. It's not a huge corner, but I'm glad Mom was able to spare the space. All I need is a few plants, a carpeted table, some brain games, and my *Inteli-Cat*. But this morning, only one thing matters—the perfection of this sunbeam. It's exactly where I want it. Not an inch out of place. I'm about to take the best nap of my life, and that's saying something. I've had some awesome naps. I'll have to go through the list later to see where this one sits.

Mom says normal cats don't rank their naps. She says most don't have an *Inteli-Cat* system either. I don't understand why. Do other cats not enjoy ranking their naps? Or watching wild animals roam the Earth? Now that Earth's gone, how else am I supposed to see the world?

Mom says I'm not like other cats. They still don't know what planet I come from, but it's definitely not Earth. I don't remember my kitten years. I get flashes sometimes when I sleep. Green all around me. Big trees, long grass, endless rivers flowing in the bright light of the sun. I've seen similar places on my *Inteli-Cat*, but nothing quite the same. They're looking, though. Mom says they get closer every day. I'd love to see where I come from. To meet other cats like me. It's been forever since I had a friend.

Mom's friends are nice, but they're humans. It just isn't the same. They all treat me like some stupid animal. Except for Lee. She treats me like a human—values my opinion. We've been friends forever. She used to take me exploring back on Earth.

Mom says my desire to explore comes from something called my 'extraterrestrial heritage'. That's just gibberish to me, but I think she's referring to my alien origins. *Extraterrestrial*. That's a funny word. I'll have to ask Mom what that means. When a question pops into my mind I have to ask. It'll bother me all week if I don't. Until another question takes its place. But nothing will replace my biggest question: Are there others like me?

Being the only cat aboard is lonely sometimes. Mom tries her best, but we can't even talk without my translator. There will always be gaps that she can't fill. That being said, Earth cats didn't cut it either. All they did is eat and sleep. I'm not against eating and sleeping, those being two of my favourite pass-times, but I wish they were more interesting. A line exists between the two—a best of both worlds situation, but I won't get that unless I find my kind. For now,

I'm stuck with humans. At least Lee's nice.

Lee is my second favourite. It goes Mom, Lee, Sean, Kasper, and then Brian. Brian's mean to everyone. I don't know why he's on the ship. Whenever I ask, Mom says it's because he's important to the mission. She won't explain why, but Brian's the one who makes fun of me the most. He always tells me they're going to drop me off at the next planet. "You're an alien, you'll make it!" Mom says he's just trying to be funny.

I'd love to explore other planets. I've volunteered to be the first one down when we reach our destination. It would give me a chance to conduct my secret investigation. Mom said no, obviously. I'll convince her, but not now. Not during this excellent sunbath.

Speaking of, a knock on my door soon interrupts my wonderful morning. I give the meow to enter and rise with an amazing stretch. I expect Mom to open the door, but it's Lee.

"Hey, Heli," she says. "How's it going?"

Meow.

"Want your *Inteli-Cat*?"

I hop to the stool in front of the touchscreen. A tap of the paw unlocks it, and brings me to the translation app.

"Good morning, Lee."

"Good morning, Helios." She scratches behind my ear. "Jeez, you're hot. I guess you're enjoying the sun."

My black and brown coat is a heat magnet. It makes getting pets hard, but the sunbath trade-off is worth it.

"I am, but I miss the real sun."

"Me too, buddy," she sighs. "It's okay. We're making progress. Any luck with your secret mission?"

I forgot I told her. I wonder if she told the others.

"No."

"That's okay." She gives me a pat on the head. I close my eyes and purr.

"Your mom wants you in the Meeting Deck," she continues.

"Why?"

"She's called a meeting with the crew. You're part of the crew, Helios."

Mom always invites me to their meetings. It's her way of making me feel like part of the team.

"Why a meeting?"

"I'm not sure. I guess we'll see. Want to go down together?"

"Sure."

She offers to carry me, but I refuse. I prefer to walk.

The Meeting Deck is at the center of the station, below the Officer's quarters, and above Storage. The cockpit is just down the hall, but I'm not allowed in there. The curiosity is killing me.

Everyone's waiting when we arrive. My spot is in between Lee and Sean, opposite from Mom. She's in charge, so she's at the head of the table. Lee takes her place, and I hop up next to her. My *Inteli-Cat* is still upstairs, but Mom installed the translator into my stool, in the event that I have something to say. Sean grins and ruffles my fur.

"How's it going?" he asks.

I meow in response.

"I'll take that as awesome," he says. He switches to Lee. "Finish those translations, yet?"

"I'm close," she says. "I…"

Mom clears her throat. Everyone falls silent.

"Good morning," she says. "Hope everyone's projects are going well. I have some good news, but first I want a status update. Lee, the translations?"

"I think I've cracked the sentence structure," says Lee. "Got most of the vowels down, just working out the rest. I should be done in a few days."

"Good," says Mom. "Kasper, any progress on the silicon hypothesis?"

Kasper straightens up from across the table, which puts him at around half the size of Sean.

"Some, I suppose," he says. "But I'm going to need samples before I can do much else."

"I understand," says Mom. "As luck has it, we might be able to get you some."

Everyone begins to rustle and chatter. I want to tell them to be quiet while Mom's speaking, but they stop on their own.

"I picked something up on the radar," she explains. "A planet."

"Are you serious?" Sean exclaims.

"I am. What's more is that I've gotten us clearance to investigate."

Noise erupts from all around me. Sean is laughing and punching the air. Next thing I know, I'm in Lee's arms as she squeezes and showers me with kisses.

"How did you manage to do that?" Kasper demands. "This is incredible, Dr. Phoenix."

"Thank you, Kasper," she says.

"Well done," says Lee.

Mom smiles.

"Thank you everyone, but congratulations are not in order yet. Not until we succeed. To do that, we'll need your help."

I assume she's addressing Lee.

"Lee, would you place Helios back on his translator?"

She's talking to me. She needs *my* help. Is this really happening?

"You need my help, Mom?"

"Yes, Helios. I need your help. We all do."

"Yeah right," Brian chuckles. "He's a cat, Elena. What can he do that we can't?"

"Not now, Brian," she snaps, which makes him fall silent. "Helios, I need you to be our eyes."

Eyes? What does she mean? She has eyes, everyone does. How could I be her eyes?

"When we reach this planet and confirm its surface temperature, atmospheric levels, and so on, I'm sending you to the surface."

"What?!" Kasper shouts. "You can't be serious."

"I am, Kasper," she hisses. "Don't raise your voice at me. I'm your captain, follow orders. Got it?"

She gives him the look. The same one she gives me when I'm caught drinking her coffee. I know it scares me; I'm not surprised when he shuts up.

"Your physiology is different from ours," she says. "You'll be safer down there. We'll give you gear, of course, but we'll pull you back up the second anything happens. You'll collect samples and scout the area. You can fit in places we can't."

"I know it's not my place," says Sean. "But this is crazy, don't you think? It'll be dangerous no matter what.

Helios, will you be able to defend yourself? To improvise?"

"I realize it's dangerous." She sighs. "If I had it my way, I'd be down there. But this is the deal. I can't get permission for a human to go down yet. Who knows how long that'll take. But Heli isn't human, so those rules don't apply."

"So, you're cheating the Government of Humanity?" Kasper demands.

"We've come this far," Mom declares, pounding her fist on the table. "Do you really want to give up now because of some stupid rules from those clueless politicians? I don't, so this is the plan. Feel free to report me, but by the time they arrive, it'll already be done. It's time to choose, everyone."

Silence spreads among the crew.

"You can count on me, Mom."

"I know, Heli. Lee?"

Lee shoots me a nervous glance. She's fiddling with the curls of her hair—a sign she's stressed.

"I'm in," she says. "But we're putting him on a line and pulling him back at the first sign of trouble."

"Of course," says Mom. "Sean?"

"Hell yeah, I'm in," he cackles. "Can't believe this little trooper's going to beat me to the surface."

"Fine," says Kasper. "I trust you, Doctor."

"Thank you," says Mom. "Brian?"

Brian folds his arms across his massive chest. His eyebrows disappear into his sandy hair.

"I ain't going to be the odd one out." He shrugs. "To hell with it. You better get the job done, cat."

"I will."

"Good," says Mom. A grin splits across her face, like none I've seen before. "Back to your stations, everyone. Helios, come with me. Let's get you prepped."

***

Helios, the first being to ever step foot on an alien planet. It has a nice ring to it.

Mom is trying to explain the mission, but I'm too excited to pay attention. I need my scratching post. I'd go crazy on that thing right about now.

"Heli, please. Settle down. I need you to focus so we can go over the plan."

Okay, I need to sit. The excitement will have to wait.

"I made you a spacesuit," she explains. "It has a bunch of gadgets, so I'll need you to run through the manual on your *Inteli-Cat* before I can let you go down."

I meow my understanding.

"Good."

She's fidgeting. Biting her nails and tapping her foot. I hop to my stool.

"What is wrong, Mom?"

"Nothing, bud," she says. "I just don't want you to get hurt. These politicians... you wouldn't understand. They're very hard on Mom, okay? I wish I was down there with you."

"I will be okay. Do not worry."

"I know, I know." She strokes my fur. Lee gives good scratches, but Mom's the only one who knows my spot. When she hits it, I'm in paradise.

"We'll be looking through a camera on your suit," she says. "We'll see what you see. Do you understand?"

"Yes, Mom."

"You'll go where we tell you to go. I know you'll want to explore, but there will be time for that later. I need you to listen to me and do exactly as I say. It's the only way I'll be able to keep you safe."

"Yes, Mom."

"We're attaching a line to your suit. If anything happens, we reel you in. It's not like the ones from the movies we watch. This one works. You'll be okay."

Why is she saying that so much? I know I'll be okay; she doesn't have to convince me.

"Mom."

"Yes, Heli?"

"Will I find others like me?"

The anticipation is excruciating. My chance is finally here.

"I don't know." She won't look at me. She's focused on the plant by my window. Is there a bug?

"I want to find them."

What a perfect life that'd be. Running in the fields with my fellow cats. Chatting, playing—learning about our history. Mom could still do her work. If there's a planet of cats, life can thrive. We could all be happy together. Just the thought makes me swell.

"I know you want to find them," she says. "I know it must be hard to be the only cat on board. We love you, Heli, and loving someone means doing what is best for them. Even if it means I have to let you go." She wipes a tear from her cheek. "If you find them, you do what your heart tells you. Remember that."

I'm not sure what she means, but I'm too wired to think about it.

"I will remember. Thank you, Mom. I love you too."

She gives me a warm smile. One she doesn't use with her friends. She wraps me in her arms, placing her chin atop my head. I nuzzle into her chest and close my eyes, listening to the mellow thump of her heart.

"I knew I could count on you, buddy."

Mom's clock reads the number eighteen by the time I finish the manual. There were some big words in there, but I think I got the gist. I'll be wearing a suit made of something called *nanotechnology*—tiny robots according to the note Mom added. These tiny robots will be the shapes of weapons and gear that I can operate using my brain. At least, that's how I took it. With the mission established and the gear ready to go, all that's left to do is wait. I never thought the day would come where I wouldn't be able to sleep.

Days upon days go by, where I sit and wait by my door, hoping Mom or Lee come in to announce we've arrived. I tried to study for at least an hour a day, but my attention span isn't long enough for that. It's not my fault that a fly got in, I had to catch it. Mom would have wanted me to. Besides, how did a fly enter our space station? Maybe they can breathe in space. I wonder if I can breathe in space. I've always wanted to try, but Mom says it's too dangerous. She would rather me wear a *respirator* just in case. I assume those help people breathe.

I wonder if I'll find any aliens. If I do, what will I say to them? If only I had a rat, I could bring along as a gift, just in case. Mom used to love it when I brought her rats. She stored them as little keep-sakes in the garage, though I'm not sure how she fit them all in that tiny container. One of Earth's many unsolved mysteries.

Mom has been very attached to me since giving me my

mission. When she's not doing work, she's in my room. We play games and watch animals on my *Inteli-Cat*. Then I curl up in her lap for a perfect grooming session. I miss the sun's heat, but nothing will ever beat the warmth of Mom's hugs. It's funny, because though she's with me all the time, she hasn't been talking much. Only a few words here and there, but she never answers when I ask about the cats I might find. She just stares at me, like she's trying to take a picture with her eyes. She's sad, and I can't figure out why. It's like she's lost something. I can't focus on that; I need to prepare for my descent. It looks like today might be the day.

A knock wakes me from my afternoon nap. Lee enters the room.

"It's time, Heli."

She escorts me downstairs like a prince. Everyone I pass gives me a pat and wishes me luck. Even Brian, who's never had a kind word to say. Maybe Mom was right. Maybe they do all love me.

We reach the cockpit where my curiosity is finally satisfied. So many buttons... so many knobs and dials to play with. Why would Mom withhold such a heavenly place? I'm itching to play. No, I can't get distracted. I have to show her that I'm disciplined or else she won't let me go. The flashing buttons will still be here when I return.

Mom and Lee are the only ones in the cockpit. It's so small, I doubt it would fit anyone else. Mom straps a harness to my back, meaning I immediately drop to the ground. I'm dying, this is so uncomfortable. It's like someone is squeezing my chest and tickling my armpits at the same time.

"Come on, Helios," Mom groans. "Don't be so dramatic."

Dramatic? Obviously, Mom has never been hoisted up by her armpits before. It takes all my strength to get back on my feet. Ignore it. Just ignore it.

"This is your suit," she explains. "When you're ready, I'll activate it, engulfing you in complete protection. You won't be able to bite anything, so if you have an itch, now's the time."

I'm glad she warned me. There's a spot just below my ear that's been bugging me all morning. I try to scratch it, but Lee eventually steps in.

"Good," Mom says. "Now, we've already landed. Kasper and I have been running data for the past twenty-four hours, and the atmosphere should be decent. That being said, still do *not* remove your suit. The temperature is cooler than Earth, but not by much. Your suit will maintain your body temperature all the same. Is that clear?"

Meow.

"Okay. Next, the plan. We're letting you out via the south exit. As I said, we'll be looking through a camera on your suit. We need soil samples from a few different locations, I'll direct you to each, but your helmet will also display points of interest—places I need you to go. Many features of your *Inteli-Cat* have been installed, in addition to programs that can run vitals. Lee even added a dialect translator based on the alien scripts we found last month. I know this is complicated stuff, but you won't be alone. I'll be talking to you the whole time, telling you exactly what to do. In the event we get disconnected, your suit will help you, along with that killer instinct of yours."

She grins and ruffles my fur.

"You can do this, Heli," Lee whispers.

"You're the strongest cat in the universe," Mom says, kissing my head. "So, are you ready?"

The pride on Mom's face makes me swell with confidence. She's right. I'm the strongest cat in the universe!

Meow.

"Great. I'll activate your suit."

She taps a button on my back. The discomfort vanishes. Instead, an aura of claustrophobia surrounds me like a tight hug. I can't really see myself, but it's clear that my whole body has been encased. Flashing colours and numbers appear on the surface of my visor. I feel like a superhero ready to explore the entire universe.

***

Mom won't let go of me. Lee and Sean have to drag her back to the safe zone in order to lower the bridge. Her eyes are red, and her skin is pale. She's scared, but she has no reason to be. I'm the strongest cat in the universe.

She nods and mouths something I can't discern. English is easy enough to understand, but I never got the hang of mouth reading.

"Good luck!" Everyone shouts, as the airlock hisses. It's time.

I'm not sure what I was anticipating, but what lies before me exceeds all expectations.

It's... beautiful. Long grass and rolling hills stretching towards the horizon. Tall trees and massive rock faces, speckled like spots of paint. I can see a waterfall in the distance. The peaceful spill is like music to my ears. There's so much green, more than I ever imagined. Something about this place sends a tingle through my fur. A familiar sense of déjà-vu. Is this where I belong?

The suit is ruining this experience. It's blocking my dark fur from absorbing these new sun rays. I can't feel the wind caressing my fur, or the soft, loamy, soil beneath my paws. I want to smell the air. Roll in the grass and take a nap. But I can't. I'm on a mission and Mom is counting on me.

"Helios? Can you hear me?"

This must be Mom speaking through my suit.

"Yes."

"Good," she says. "How are you doing?"

"I am doing good. This place is wonderful. I wish I could feel the wind."

"If you get the right samples, maybe you'll be able to," she says. "This is only the first step. But you're right..." she sighs. "It is beautiful. This is it, buddy. We did it."

"We did."

"Are you ready for your first stop?"

Mom directs me through the valley, with little dots appearing on my visor to guide me to sample locations. At every stop, I use the "soil" tool to scoop a load and store it in the compartments on my legs. By the third try, I'm nearing the cliffside. The waterfall is barely fifty meters away, according to my visor.

"Great work," says Mom. "You're doing wonderful. I just need a water sample, now. Can you get one from that waterfall?"

"Yes."

"Amazing. Remember, you're still connected through the cord. If you're in trouble, say so, and we'll pull you back."

I'm surprised the string hasn't gotten in my way. The thin line is trailing behind me like a power cord, running hundreds of meters back to the ship.

I know I'm supposed to go straight to the waterfall, but I can't help but stray to the edge of the cliff. The light brown cliffside runs a hundred meters down, according to my suit. They say cats always land on their feet, but that fall would certainly kill me. Unless I landed in the pond. The water is so clear, I can see the reflection of the sky. It reminds me of a lake we visited back on Earth. The only time I got to ride a plane.

I walk along the edge, despite Mom's warnings that I'm getting too close. I have excellent balance. When I reach the small cave beneath the waterfall, the noise drowns out Mom's voice, but that's okay. I know what to do. As the manual said, I use the "water" tool to take a sample from the downpour. It goes into a storage unit on my belly, so that it won't get ruined. All that's left is to return to the ship. But before I can turn back, something catches my eye. An inscription on the cave wall. Mom's voice is cutting in and out.

"...Heli... volume."

She wants me to turn up her volume.

"Heli, can you hear me?"

"Yes."

"Whew," she sighs. "Remember what the manual said about loud noises? You have to turn up my voice."

"Sorry, Mom."

"It's okay, you figured it out. That sample will do, but what's that on the rock?"

"Writing."

Whispers echo through my suit. Then, Lee speaks for the first time.

"Helios, can you get closer? Try using my dialect tool."

I edge closer to the writing, which has been carved into the stone. It's only one line, and it definitely isn't English. I switch on Lee's dialect tool. Letters pop up on my visor, below the inscription. It can't translate the whole thing, but one word is complete.

"Cat."

"What was that, Heli?"

"It says *cat*."

More whispers.

"Oh my God, you're right," Lee gasps. "It takes a minute to receive the data, but you're right. You know what that means, Elena?"

"Life."

I'm so excited, I nearly slip off the edge. Life… there's life here. There are cats. Maybe this is what I've been looking for, all this time. There has to be more—another clue. I sniff the cave wall for any hint of a fellow feline.

"Unauthorized scan. Danger. Danger."

My helmet is speaking to me.

"Helios, what's going on?" Mom demands. "Helios?"

Before I can make sense of what's happening, a crack appears in the rock. If there's one thing I'm good at, it's opening doors I'm not supposed to. I wedge my head in the space, and it swings open.

"Elena!" Lee exclaims. "He found something!"

"Helios, talk to me," says Mom. "Tell me what you see."

"A room." My heart flutters, sweeping me off my feet. "A room of cats."

It really is as simple as that. I've stumbled upon a small cavern featuring a table of eight or nine cats, all of which are staring at me.

"Cats? Elena, he's right. Look!"

"Helios, are you okay?" Mom asks.

"Yes. I want to talk to them."

As I get closer, I realize they aren't mirror images of the cats I know. They're bigger—stronger. They have wise eyes, and silky fur. The most elite felines I've ever seen. The one at the head of the table is the most intimidating, with a blood-red coat and violet eyes. Intimidating, yet beautiful. When she looks over it makes my fur tingle. She speaks first.

"Who are you?" she asks.

"I am Helios."

"Heli, are you talking to them?" Mom asks, but Lee shushes her.

"Greetings Helios," they all meow in unison.

"You passed our DNA scan," says the leader. "You must be a cat. Where do you come from?"

Mom would want me to say Earth—to bargain for her people. But I can't lie, not to this cat.

"I do not know," I say. "But my crew is from Earth."

"Hm." She meows to the cat next to her. "We have not heard of this Earth. Is it far?"

"Yes," I say. "We have been traveling for many years since climate change made our planet uninhabitable."

"I see."

"Who are *you*?" I ask. "What planet is this?"

"My name is Clover, and we are the Council of Cats," she says. "This planet has been our home ever since the people died."

"People? Humans lived here?"

"I am unfamiliar with the term *human*," she says. "But maybe."

"What do you seek, Helios?" asks another cat. This one is grey and black with stormy eyes, and sharp whiskers. The type I'd scrap with on the block.

"We seek a home," I say. "The Government of Humanity needs a new place for us to live."

More chatter. Too quiet to understand. My heart is beating out of my chest. I've prepared for this. I can't screw it up.

"Come here, Helios," says Clover.

The purr in her voice makes it impossible to disobey. She hops down to meet me, her wise eyes boring a hole through my soul.

"I would like to show you something," she says. "Take my seat."

She doesn't attempt to sniff me, as if she already knows what she'll find. I hop to her stool.

"Paka, initiate the relocation."

A sandy cat at the other end places his paw on the slick tabletop. A moment later, the surface is replaced by a series of images—waves of colour and darkness. Shapes dancing in shadow. There's no physical sense to them. Only emotion... a feeling. A world without people. Heart-racing, curiosity-driven freedom.

"Elena, what's he watching?"

I lower their volume. They might not understand, but I do.

"You are a cat," says Clover. "You belong here, with your kind. I will allow you to stay—to make a home for yourself on our planet."

"I can stay?"

"You can. But your *humans* may not."

"My mom can't stay?" I ask. "Why?"

Clover leaps up next to me and rubs against my suit. Even through my tiny robots, I can feel her warmth.

"We cats have ruled this planet for over a thousand years," says Clover. "I, myself, have been the leader for over a hundred. People held us back for centuries. We were their pets. Now, we are free."

"Free?" I ask.

"Free," she purrs. "We have spent years building a society for the better of our kind. We put all cats first because all cats deserve to live the best of lives."

"Even me?"

"Even you."

I can't feel my whiskers. Numbness spreads through my body, digging a hole where my heart should be. After all this time, all this effort. The dreams and the fantasies. They're making me choose.

"This is not fair," I say. "My mom is good. Can she stay?"

"I'm sorry, Helios. We do not know her government's intensions and we do not make exceptions. You must choose. Will you leave your humans behind for the better of catkind?"

The thump of her heart against my chest reminds me of Mom—of how she hugged me before I left. The tears that ran from her eyes.

"Helios?" Mom's voice is barely audible. "Helios, please answer. We can't understand you, are you okay? Mom's worried buddy. Please come back. We can find a new home."

"Elena, let him speak," says Lee.

"I just need him to know," says Mom. Her voice cracks. "I love you, buddy. If this is your kind... your family... then you should stay."

Mom has stopped talking, but I can hear her hyperventilating. She's scared. Mom is never scared. I listen to Clover's heart—to the thump of freedom at the tip of my nose. But what she said about putting her people first gives me an itch. It's the same thing Mom said. It's what she's doing for me. Suddenly the thumping changes. A heartbeat without the love I get with every one of Mom's hugs. The flutter inside me vanishes and my own heart begins to ache. I know what I must do.

"I am sorry, Clover," I say. "But the life you describe would be nothing without my mom. I must go back."

I jump down.

"Are you sure?"

"I am."

"I see," says Clover. "So be it. People are our downfall, Helios. They will hold you back. Remember that."

"Maybe, but I will find out for myself. I love my mom. I cannot leave her."

"Very well."

The crew won't be happy if they hear we're back to stage one. My mission is to collect data, so that's what I'm going to do.

"Clover."

"Yes, Helios."

"I know we cannot live here, but would you lend me your knowledge of this galaxy? My mom and I need a home, even if it is not here."

"Normally I would reject such a request," says Clover. "But whether you live with humans or not, you are a cat. We must respect our own kind. Does everyone agree?"

Meows of assent circle the table.

"Good," she says. "We used to be part of a space colony before the people died out. There are five other planets within this colony, all of which had life. We do not know if life still resides on these planets, but that is for you to discover."

"Thank you," I say. "I will tell my mom."

"Do as you wish. Farewell, Helios. Good luck with your mission."

"Goodbye Clover."

She leans in and sniffs my nose. A gesture of good will, which I return.

"Helios?" Mom asks. "Are you leaving? Are you coming back?"

"I am coming home, Mom. See you soon."

***

"I don't see why we can't just wipe them out," Brian is arguing.

"We will not wipe out another species for our gain," says Mom.

"They're only cats," Brian counters.

"They are smarter than you," I say.

The Meeting Deck goes silent.

"Excuse me?" Brian snaps.

"They are smarter than you, Brian," I repeat. "They have ruled this planet for over a thousand years, and they are still alive. They have grown beyond the need for human care."

"Is that so," says Brian. "Then why didn't you stay, huh? If it's so much better than humanity."

"That's enough, Brian," Mom hisses. "You will not talk to him like that. Helios just pulled off the most important mission in human history. We owe him everything."

"Most important mission?" Brian laughs. "We're back to stage one, Elena. That accomplished nothing."

"Actually, you're wrong," says Kasper. All eyes turn to him. He flushes and shoves his glasses up the bridge of his nose. "The samples we collected are invaluable. We can now study these and potentially reevaluate our core principles of what life needs to survive. Carbon levels, oxygen levels, nutrients, the whole lot. It'll take a while, but I'm certain I'll reach a conclusion."

"Thank you, Kasper," says Mom. "With our samples, and the knowledge Heli gained from those cats, we have a plan. We have five other planets to explore, all of which gave rise to life. One of them will work."

"You're so sure?" Brian demands.

"I am. So, are you going to continue complaining or are we going to get to work? Humanity won't save itself."

He scoffs and folds his arms but doesn't reply. Mom turns to me.

"Excellent work, Helios." She chuckles. "Just a planet of cats, eh Brian? Look what *one* just did for humanity."

She strides over and lifts me into her arms.

"Thanks for coming back, buddy," she whispers.

I purr and nuzzle between her neck. I'm not on my translator, but I don't need it. She knows my answer.

Living Bad Dreams
By Denise Hatfield

When dreams come alive, there's no telling where they will lead. Everything changes when you realize that, dream or no dream, you're going to die. What do you do then?

Ordering Link:
Print Edition: https://www.hiraethsffh.com/product-page/living-bad-dreams-by-denise-hatfield-1

ePub edition: https://www.hiraethsffh.com/product-page/living-bad-dreams-by-denise-hatfield-2

The Lost Unicorn
Lisa Voorhees

When Edvard first sighted the bedraggled creature stumbling across the Grenmark Expanse, he believed it to be a feral horse, separated from its herd. Darkness shadowed the tundra this time of year. Winter lasted a full six months, and what muted light did exist blurred the boundary between the edge of the forest and the horizon.

He swiped a hand over his wind-chapped face and picked ice pellets from his thick beard. The animal teetered this way and that, hooves soundlessly pockmarking the landscape. Head hung low, it swept the ground as if in hopes of catching a stray blade of vegetation piercing through the snow cover.

Mercenary work had trained Edvard to survive whatever the wilderness threw at him; ice fishing in his isolated retirement ensured he stayed in practice. His instincts told him to quit fishing, pack up his gear, and seek shelter from the fierce winds; the creature would either find a way to survive, or it wouldn't.

Edvard stopped mid-stride.

The rescue of one starved horse would never make up for the hundreds of men he had slain in battle as a mercenary, but perhaps it was one small way of cutting through the darkness. Acting on his conscience would not be counted against him out here, not like it had in battle.

As if aware of his thoughts, the creature glanced up, nostrils quivering in the wind. Edvard stared at the handbreadth of space between its ears.

This was no wild horse.

The horned creature stared back at him, exhaustion and fear swirling in the depths of its dark, haunted eyes. A unicorn. Its chest heaved like a bellows. Bursts of mist blossomed from its nose. Its knees buckled; the frozen ground creaked.

Nothing short of a dying man's avarice could have induced a creature of the Southlands this far north. King

Heidenstam's condition must be deteriorating, causing him to lust for the miraculous healing properties of the unicorn's horn. Edvard suspected the king's hunters would not be far behind.

Another faltering misstep in the permafrost and the unicorn could break a limb, or worse. The Grenmark was riddled with deep pits. Geothermal gas bubbles rose to the surface and created air pockets in the ice cover; Edvard had grown accustomed to giving the darkened ice above those holes a wide berth.

The fisherman whistled–a high, keening sound like the song of the blue-gray bitfly. A Southern species of woodland bird, and one that would be familiar to the unicorn.

The distressed creature rolled an eye toward him, its neck bowed as if under the weight of a heavy yoke. The dying light of the sinking sun stained its white flanks orange, followed by a burnt crimson. The points of its hips protruded painfully above the flesh. The unicorn would not survive another night on the frigid plains.

Edvard removed a length of rope from an inner pocket of his coat and held the coil loosely in one hand. Slow and steady was the key; a starved, frightened creature would preserve its energy until the last possible moment, then bolt.

"I won't hurt you, beauty," he said, his tone low and soothing. "Come. We need to get you somewhere safe." He approached the unicorn cautiously.

The great dark eyes examined him. Edvard hesitated, allowing the animal to smell the rope in his hand. The unicorn backed up a step, withers trembling.

"I live a little further that way." Edvard tipped his head in the direction of his hut. "There's a cleft in the rocks, over yonder. Protection from the wind, and good food. What do you say?"

He gently slung the looped end of the rope over the unicorn's head. The creature ducked, snorting harshly.

Edvard chuckled. "Okay. How do you propose we do this, then? I don't want you turning a leg in the pits."

The unicorn eyed him. A glimmer of light passed through its eyes, then vanished.

My name is Wynstar. I trust you to help me.

Awareness of the unicorn's voice flooded Edvard's mind, and warmth crept into the marrow of his bones. To know a unicorn's name was to wield power over it. The creatures were not known to reveal their identities to any but their own kind and the forest sprites who guarded the woodlands.

Edvard crossed his hand over his heart and inclined his head to the beast. "I will not betray your trust," he said, lifting his head to meet the unicorn's intelligent gaze. "I swear to you, on my life."

They picked their way over the frozen ground, and Edvard was careful to point out every pit. The unicorn followed him at a slow walk. The darkened entrance to the cave appeared ahead. Edvard led the way through the narrow opening. The unicorn turned in a small circle, visibly relieved when at last he could sink into the deep bed of straw Edvard scattered for him.

Though he munched through a bushel of hay and wolfed down several handfuls of grain, the unicorn appeared weaker after having eaten than he did out on the plains. His neck lolled to one side, barely able to support the weight of his head.

Edvard crouched next to the unicorn and laid his hand against the creature's flesh. An icy chill snaked through his fingers. He yanked his hand away and lit another torch, bending closer to gaze at the animal.

Sunlight, he thought to himself. The notable difference between the cave shelter and the frozen tundra was the scant remaining bit of sunlight the unicorn had been able to absorb out on the fields. No wonder he had balked at being brought inside. He lived on light, and not on food alone.

Edvard stretched out his back and sighed. It was a month's journey to the Southlands from the Grenmark Expanse. If he was sighted by any of the king's men, he could be forced into service. He wasn't duplicitous enough to pull off a disguise; his scarred face was too recognizable. He'd buried himself in the Grenmark to shed the weight of his guilt, but what was a life spent scratching out his survival in the ice when this one small shot at redemption presented itself?

He could put his livelihood on hold to care for the unicorn if it meant delaying the spread of Heidenstam's corruption.

He would need to pack sparingly, and be quick about it. They would leave at the first sign of light in the morning.

***

A dark cloud lined the horizon. Edvard squinted through the window of his hut, then thumbed his eyes and glanced out again. No, not a cloud. A line of riders. A contingent of the king's men, no doubt.

He kicked the bags he had packed under his cot and made a quick weapons sweep of the hut, ensuring his knives were all on his person. He grasped the leather pouch at his neck and tucked it under his shirt. Escape was no option, not with a weakened unicorn in tow.

A fierce battering shook the door on its hinges. "Open up for inspection! King's orders!"

Edvard released the catch on the handle and the door shuddered open. A company of five soldiers stood on the other side, the commander in front. They'd tethered their mounts near his woodpile, along with a covered transport wagon. Dark capes swept back from their shoulders, and fur hats sat low over their ears.

"I am Chief Inspector Orvar. Who are you?"

"A fisherman."

The commander's gaze passed over Edvard, contemptuous and cold. Slowly, he removed his gloves; his mink's eyes narrowed to slits. "Don't I know you?"

The scar that ran beneath Edvard's eye and down his cheek burned, but he remained silent, impassive. If he was lucky, Orvar would consider him simple, his lack of response nothing more than ignorance.

The commander snapped the gloves against his wrist, his dark eyes flashing. "Edvard Nordane. The mercenary."

Edvard paused. Orvar was sharper than he anticipated.

"Retired, and no longer for hire." He wasn't one for pretending.

Orvar's chuckle held cruelty. "What does the Grenmark have to offer you, hmm?" He strolled inside the hut, pausing to examine the fishing equipment hanging from the four walls and stowed away in the corners. He gave the nearest bucket a swift kick. "Ice fishing? Can that be enough to sustain an appetite for blood such as yours?"

The reminder stung but Edvard stifled his wrath. The soldiers moved freely about the hut, poking into corners and searching every stored item they got their hands on.

An excited shout from one of them drew Orvar's attention to the bags stashed under the cot. The commander inspected the contents, then turned to face Edvard, a sneer on his lips.

Edvard didn't flinch.

"Planning a trip?" the inspector said.

"I always keep my bags packed in case of storms." He was calm, despite the rage within.

Orvar scoffed. "You would not live in the Grenmark if you feared the storms. Care to try again, this time with the truth?"

"Larger game to hunt in the Far North." Edvard maintained a steady gaze.

"I see." Orvar considered him closely. By the corner of his eye, a twitch started. His fingers sought the hilt of the sword at his waist.

Edvard made no move to reach for his hidden weapons.

The commander's hand stilled. A moment later, he snapped his fingers for his mens' attention. "We will shelter here for the next twenty-four hours," he said, pinning his dark, malicious gaze on Edvard, "in order to complete our inspection."

So, they were commandeering his hut. Edvard quietly sucked air in through his teeth. He must brace himself for difficulty, starting with a show of hospitality. He reached for a bottle of whiskey, then lined up the few tin cups he had on the table, his back to the soldiers, the majority of whom had stepped outside to recover their packs from their mounts.

A hard pinch on his elbow stopped him from pouring the next drink.

"If I find you have been hiding anything important from King Heidenstam, you understand the repercussions, don't you?" Orvar drank and slammed the cup on the table.

Calmly, Edvard refilled it.

Orvar sniffed. "Your past talents would prove of great service to the king."

Edvard held his breath and willed himself not to react. Forced conscription for Heidenstam would be a fate worse than death. The bodies would pile up by day, the screams in his mind at night, the darkness tightening its grip around him so he could hardly breathe.

He waited until Orvar swept past the door. Then he released a long, shuddering sigh, pulled out the pouch hidden under his shirt, and emptied a pinch of the contents into each of the cups.

***

The powder took effect in under an hour. The company of soldiers, including Orvar, lay asleep inside their bedrolls or slumped forward on the table, snoring in their chairs. Edvard closed the door soundlessly behind him and slipped into the soft afternoon light of the cleft between the rocks.

At the sound of his footfall, the unicorn raised his head, his eyes dull with exhaustion. Edvard pressed an apple to the creature's lips. The unicorn nibbled at the skin, gave a soft huff, then bit down weakly.

Edvard rolled onto the straw by the unicorn's side. "There has been a delay," he said, his voice rough and dry. "Heidenstam's men have arrived. They searched the hut. I'm not sure how long I can keep them from discovering you."

He hoped the unicorn would read the sentiment off his heart, the one too painful to speak. Edvard needed absolution, not the looming threat of more killing. The unicorn's survival hung on a tenuous thread, but Edvard was willing to risk himself for the creature if it would ease the burden of guilt on his soul.

A stray shaft of light shone through a crack in the rock wall. It illuminated the pure white fringe of the unicorn's eyelashes, the tips of which glimmered silver in the sun's pale glow.

"I never go back on a promise," Edvard continued. "We will find a way out of this." He touched the unicorn's nose, dismayed at the frigidity of the creature's flesh.

"If they find you, they will kill you for your horn, and I will be forced to kill for the king."

The unicorn gazed at him.

Unsure the creature understood the depth of his concern, Edvard explained. "When I came to the Grenmark, I made a promise to myself. No more bloodshed. I will never kill again, or be responsible for another's death."

He wished the unicorn would speak into his mind again, offer some consolation that he had half a chance of succeeding while abiding by his promises.

Perhaps the creature was too weary for speech. Or perhaps he considered Edvard a lost cause. "You are weak. Please eat. You need your strength." Edvard rotated the apple in his palm.

"I have drugged the king's men," he continued. "It won't give us the lead time we need to start out for the Southlands, but it's enough for you to flee deeper into the Grenmark. There are caves aplenty scattered throughout the Barren Hills northwest of here. Mind the pits, and you'll be safe enough. I will find you when this is over."

The unicorn shifted in the bed of straw. With considerable effort, he heaved himself onto unsteady legs and shook out his mane. He took one trembling step toward Edvard and hesitated, as if testing his own strength.

Edvard rose, mesmerized by the swirling dust surrounding the creature. The particles glimmered like sparks of sunlight on a layer of freshly fallen snow. The unicorn approached him and touched the tip of his horn to Edvard's chest, directly over his heart.

The fisherman froze, praying the unicorn wouldn't skewer him.

"I should never have taken you in," Edvard murmured. "Your chances with the king's men out in the Grenmark were dismal, but here you're a trapped animal, at the mercy of the human who meant to rescue you. I am sorry."

Edvard raised his arms in surrender. Death at the behest of a revered creature such as Wynstar wasn't what he had anticipated, but such an act might mean the salvation of his blackened soul.

I have no intention of taking your life, Wynstar spoke into his mind. *Forgiveness is freedom, Edvard. Remember that.*

Where the unicorn's horn touched Edvard's skin, it buzzed with warmth, spreading deep inside his chest. His pulse quickened. Layers of darkness dropped away from his heart like shed scales, the ash of them evanescing with the intensity of the unicorn's effort.

Edvard's vision tunneled, so lost was he in the experience of the unicorn's power. His darkness fought against Wynstar's light, robbing Edvard of breath. It was a shimmer of hope he had never expected to experience again. He hardly noticed when Wynstar stumbled backward, nor when a soldier's strong arm caught him about the throat, knocking the last traces of wind from his chest.

"Thought you could get away with poisoning us all, did you?" the soldier growled in his ear.

"It...wasn't...poison," Edvard gasped. He clawed at the man's arm, then stomped on the soldier's foot and drove the side of his boot into the man's shin.

With a howl, the soldier doubled over, then just as quickly recovered himself and delivered a crushing blow just below Edvard's ribs. He scruffed Edvard by the back of his collar and shoved his own face in close. "Lucky for Orvar, I don't drink whiskey," he sneered, "and I carry a phial of laurel root extract that reverses even the worst cases of intoxication. Now that everyone's awake, let's bring your little secret out into the open, shall we?" His knife snicked out of the scabbard at his side and glittered in the air between them.

"Orvar is anxious to lay eyes on the animal. You are outnumbered. I would advise you not to create a scene," the soldier threatened.

Edvard glanced at the unicorn. The creature stood in the farthest corner of the makeshift stall, his dark eyes full of tranquility. Faced with the likelihood of a fight to the death, the unicorn exuded all the calm of a quiet lake.

Panic thrilled through Edvard at the thought of leaving the unicorn. One last reassurance that he wouldn't go back on his promises was all he desired, but he couldn't get the words out.

The soldier spun him around roughly, jabbed the point of his knife into Edvard's back, and forced him outside the cavern. At the entrance to the cleft, the soldier hesitated behind him.

Thick gray clouds lined the horizon and blotted out what scant sunlight angled over the ice fields at this hour of the morning. The nearby knot of the soldiers' horses grew restless; their nervous whinnies pierced the air.

Like the gentle tinkle of falling glass, the first ice pellets hit the frozen earth. Miniscule in diameter now, at the height of the storm, they would swell to ten times the size. The ice pellets of Grenmarkian storms were legendary; the largest was reported to split a man's skull in two.

Edvard smiled to himself. The soldiers were already slipping on the frozen pellets, their flat-soled military issue boots no match for the storm-slicked ground of the Expanse.

"Hurry up!" Orvar ordered. "Bring out the beast and load it into the wagon."

The soldiers quarreled with him, pointing at the horizon.

"Do as I say," the commander countered, "or that man will kill us all before the day is through. Is he shackled?"

He cast a malignant gaze at Edvard, then thumped forward to check for himself.

One soldier raced through the cleft with a vicious looking halter, all leather and spikes with a metal cone to fit over the horn, presumably to further weaken the unicorn's power.

When Orvar produced a set of heavy iron manacles, Edvard was ready for him. He snatched a knife from inside his coat and slashed the commander's wrist. The manacles hit the ground with a dull thud. Orvar grasped his bloodied arm and stared at Edvard in horror. Despite the laurel root extract, his reflexes apparently hadn't completely recovered.

The same soldier that had rushed into the cavern now fought with the unicorn at the bottom of the ramp that led inside the covered transport wagon. Harsh spikes dug into the tender flesh around the base of his horn. Blood dripped onto the snow, fresh red petals spreading along the ice.

The unicorn balked and stamped his hooves, the whites of his eyes rolling into view underneath the dark leather straps of the halter. The soldier whipped his flanks raw, but the unicorn braced his legs, thrashed his entrapped horn in defiance, and refused to board the ramp.

Edvard was surrounded by well-armed soldiers. Orvar unsheathed his sword and advanced toward him. The fisherman barely parried his blow. His shortknife was no match for the commander's broadsword beyond one lucky defensive maneuver. He retreated in a wide half-circle and breezed past the side of the hut, where he dislodged a harpoon from its hooks.

Edvard brandished the harpoon, spinning and stabbing ruthlessly, taking on as many as three men at a time. The harpoon hummed through the air, a blood smeared, death-dealing weapon that simultaneously served as an instrument of defense.

He took a deep sword thrust to the side, close to his kidney. Edvard gritted his teeth against the surge of pain and fought harder.

Ice pellets hit the frozen earth and shattered, scattering glass-like shards underfoot. One soldier slipped and never recovered; a halo of red-stained ice encircled his head, expanding outward in an ever darkening scarlet pool.

Only Orvar remained standing. Edvard paused to catch his breath.

The unicorn stood, chest heaving, by the base of the ramp, wearied from his own struggle and the cruel halter inhibiting his power. His gaze was pinned on Edvard.

I would heal you if I could.

The unicorn's words lanced through him, warmer than a fresh sword cut to his skin. Jagged forks of lightning danced across the horizon, thunder rumbled, and underfoot, the ice shards trembled in response.

The unicorn glanced up at the sky, nostrils flared. He whickered softly, then tossed his head.

Orvar's sword whistled at Edvard from out of nowhere. A sharp pain above his heart sent Edvard reeling. The thrown blade had cracked against his rib and penetrated flesh; blood gushed down his chest. His knees hit the ice, and his vision blurred. The harpoon clattered next to him and skidded to one side.

Orvar reached for his fallen broadsword. He yanked the rope on the unicorn's halter and worked the sword under the leather strap, presumably in an attempt to unshackle and dehorn the unicorn himself.

Edvard half-stumbled, half-crawled toward them, struggling to gain purchase on the blood-slicked ice.

The ice pellets fell harder, and Orvar slipped. In a frenzied effort to recover his balance, the edge of his sword came up against the restrictive metal cone of the halter. A blinding flash of light descended from the sky. The unicorn reared up with a wild, unearthly scream. The lightning channeled through the metal cone and into Orvar's sword.

The commander seized once, then tumbled silently to the ground. In his lifeless grip, the incinerated halter was a tangle of charred leather and melted metal.

Edvard's gaze fell to Orvar's crumpled body, then traveled up to the unicorn.

The creature's hide shone the color of quicksilver, his muscles rippling with newfound strength. Silvered hooves sliced through the air and his dark eyes gleamed with preternatural light. The white of his mane flowed around him like fresh spume riding the crest of the ocean's waves. Blue streaks of electricity shot up and down the length of his horn, which glistened like a crystal spire atop his proud head.

The electric waves quieted, and a blinding light shone from the tip of the unicorn's horn. In the light of his transformation, Wynstar glowed so brightly Edvard was forced to lower his head.

Weakened and bleeding, he humbled himself on the icy ground before the animal.

You saved my life, Edvard. In return, I will grant you one wish.

The fisherman shifted on his knees, gasping for breath. He had not done nearly enough. They'd been one lightning strike away from Edvard failing to keep his promise to protect the unicorn, and five men were dead by his harpoon.

The unicorn's gaze bore into him.

Warm shimmers radiated the length of Edvard's spine. The creature could heal him physically, without a doubt, but bodily restoration was not what he longed for most.

"Please," he said, grasping the sides of his head. "Release me from the terrible darkness of this guilt. There is nowhere I can go to escape the torment of it. I cannot face what I have done. I would rather die."

A great light flashed around him, blinding Edvard to the sight of even his own body. He was adrift in a sea of lights, twinkling like stars around him.

Look around you. What do you see?

"Lights. Thousands upon thousands of them, blotting out the darkness."

Not lights, child. SOULS.

Edvard spun sideways one direction, then the other. The twinkling lights extended into infinity, no matter which way he focused.

The innocent people whom you have now saved from an evil king's rule far outnumber the lives you sacrificed in battle. Remember that.

A cold wind snapped around him, and Edvard opened his eyes. The frozen pellets had reduced to a fine, misted rain. His fingers dug into the ice-chipped soil of the Grenmark, his knuckles bruised and aching. Fresh blood dripped from his brow.

Unearthly light glowed around him. The unicorn had not left him yet. Wind whipped through his hair and whistled over the vast expanse of the Grenmark. Past the clouded rim of his vision, Edvard picked out the bodies of the fallen soldiers littering the earth.

The wind snatched at their cloaks and, the longer he watched, the less distinct their outlines became. Edvard squinted in disbelief. Their bodies were turning to ash, one by one, the dust of each spiraling into the air and twisting away, flung wide to the most distant regions of the Grenmark.

He raised his eyes to the unicorn. The great beast stood before him, serene, and dug one sharpened hoof across the ice, leaving behind a silvery trail shaped like a sword.

The unicorn whinnied once, then tossed his magnificent mane in the air. Fully energized, he pivoted on his hooves and headed at a full gallop toward the mountain pass that led to the Southlands.

Edvard staggered to his feet, his wounds screaming with the effort, as well as the joy, of his newfound freedom. His heart felt light as a bird, ready to take wing inside his chest.

With his next soft sigh, the fisherman's breath crystallized in front of his face. The storm had ended, and he had forgiven himself. Deep in the frozen waters of the Grenmark, the fish would be teeming.

From the mind of K. S. Hardy . . .

The tales of K. S. Hardy blend Grimm and Poe in a heady mix of dark and strange. From "Sometimes Above the Trees" to "The Snake's Defense," and all points in between, Hardy takes you on a tour through the unexpected and the inexplicable. Have a seat, put your feet up . . . and leave all the lights on.

https://www.hiraethsffh.com/product-page/weaving-the-light-by-k-s-hardy

Music Appreciation
Lindsey Duncan

Dossian Braeth made a show of studying his surroundings, hoping if he stalled long enough, she would come up with the answer and save him from admitting ignorance. The dislocation spell had swept them away from their pursuers, but they had been unable to control the destination. He was fairly sure it was his fault.

"Idiri! That's Idiri below us," Callia Ruis said, relief flitting across a face still pinched ruby with the cold of Neve Pass. They stood on a cliff overlooking the pale blue city, its painted buildings splashing up against the sea.

Dossian had never seen the ocean, and it was the only thing that could have torn his gaze from the redheaded woman at his side. Her dark eyes might be deeper than the waves, but that was a known wonder; the endless expanse was something new.

"Idiri," he repeated. "That's a great place to do …" He wobbled on the edge of a verbal chasm. "… whatever it is we need to do."

Callia closed her eyes. "I don't know," she said. "So much has changed. I still want justice, but we're hundreds of miles from the city of Trest and the Snowweavers, with nothing in our arsenal. The Snowweavers have to pay in blood." Her fingers tensed, digging into her palms hard enough to cut. Her face vibrated with the need for action.

Dossian cleared his throat, then realized he had nothing sensible to say. In her crusade, she had destroyed the spell restraining the winter storms in Neve Pass and fought an entire academy of rhythmists to a standstill. If her tremendous efforts had caused only mayhem – and they had – what hope was there now? He rather hoped he could convince her to not have a purpose.

Callia's visible struggle ended in stillness. She exhaled, her hands opening. She took his arm, leaning in to kiss his ear. "Let's go, Doss."

First, however, they had to strip, bundled in far too many layers for comfort. Callia stared at the sheer quantity of clothing that came off Dossian. The coat left his blond hair standing up in spikes.

"How in the world did you even manage to walk like that, much less fight?" she asked.

He smiled weakly. "Talent?"

She laughed. "All is revealed."

A path cut down the cliff and meandered through one of the city's lesser gates. Dampness clung to Idiri, breathing on the air, dusting its streets. People hurried past in flowing skirts and pantaloons, surrounded by their own private oceans.

Callia led the way towards the docks district, rough-hewn piers made for common traders and privateers. It was a midnight-dark district even in daylight, shadows cast over black-blue paint.

She never faltered, even though he would have liked to. He silently made his mission to protect and support her. It was more purpose than he had shouldered in a long time, his attempts to graduate as a rhythmist notwithstanding.

He was a rhythmist now, a fully trained spellcaster. He hadn't even gotten the lowest marks on the exam.

Callia paused in front of a tavern. She wrinkled her nose, sniffing the briny air. "Do you have any money?"

"I suited up for battle," he reminded her. "It's not as if we were going to flip a coin to decide the winner."

She frowned. "We'll ask some questions and leave. And hope they don't throw us out for not buying anything."

He peered up at the battered sign, trying to discern if the dried fluid on it was blood. "Are you sure it's safe?"

"No. But people in this kind of place mind their own business, and we might be able to find out where the work is." She set her jaw and swept inside.

Dossian scuttled after, trying not to choke on the smoky air. People grumbled at tables, old war stories or complaints about taxes. Several eyes followed them; they were younger than anyone else here, even the sallow servers circling with trays. Round-faced, nut-skinned, he felt instantly out of place in the crowd.

"Split up," Callia said. "Two pairs of ears."

He bristled, worried about leaving her. Ridiculous. She would only be paces away. To reassure her and indirectly himself, he squeezed her hand. "Good hunting."

She flashed him the sun's own smile, then headed for the bar. He wandered, possessed of no clear plan and – as he scanned the crowds – not seeing any place among them that looked terribly inviting.

The skeletal skitter of dice on wood caught his attention. He peered over towards the players, a coarse native and a tall, slim gentleman with coppery skin and fine leather gloves. This second figure looked as if he belonged, humbly dressed and hoarding a mug of ale, but the gloves stood out. Dossian was obscurely proud of himself for noticing.

The stranger's startling grey eyes flicked up and stared straight at him. Dossian flushed and made to retreat, but the man beckoned.

Resisting the urge to canvas his surroundings for whoever the man was actually summoning, Dossian inched forward. "Can I help you with something, sir?"

"Sir." The man chuckled. "You'll excuse us, won't you?" he said to his companion.

The other snorted and snapped up the coins on the table. "Your loss." He rose and slipped out.

The gloved man tipped his head to the empty chair. Dossian plopped down. "Noriak Lightshawl," the man said.

Dossian opened his mouth to speak, then shut it again. Word of their flight could not possibly have traveled already, but they didn't need to be leaving a trail. "It's, ah, Danth. Brisby."

"Well ... Danth," Noriak allowed himself the slightest smile, but it was an expression of confederacy rather than mockery, "you have the look of the wanderer about you. One a bit hard on his luck?"

"That might be," he said.

"I have a proposition for you," Noriak continued. "My family is Varhinese nobility. They once had an outpost in the area. The ruin lies a short distance south. In those ruins lie a great many things, including painful memories – and an ancient flute, an heirloom of my family. I would pay handsomely to have it retrieved."

Dossian blinked. "Why don't you do it yourself?" he asked, then winced at how the words had come out.

Noriak chuckled. "I am not a hands-on man. Coming down here is as dirty as I get. I had hoped to hire a dockhand or local guard, but none of them have that glint to their eyes. Oh, there is some danger, of course. Wild beasts camped in the ruins and such not."

Dossian swallowed. "I've faced worse." In point of fact, the only opponent he had faced was Callia, but that was more than enough. The academy had thought they could rely on him to defeat her, and instead, he had joined her. "What's the, er, compensation?"

"I'm sure you have." The lack of doubt in Noriak's voice was astonishing, and the number he quoted was even more so. "Will you do it? There isn't much time. Someone else could go seeking it at any moment."

This was precisely what they were looking for, and Noriak seemed trustworthy, unlike the strange, shifty figures around him. "Yes."

The man grinned. "Thank you, young master Brisby. Thank you."

Feeling like he might actually be the master of something, Dossian rose and started towards the bar. Callia leaned against it, conversing with the barkeep. He kept his distance until she pulled away.

"The isles are looking for rhythmists," she said as he approached, "but that means staying here for days until we can find the right ship, doing nothing." The exasperation snapped in her voice. He thought, from her expression, she would explode if she had to remain still. "To the west, rebellion. To the south, the new Varhinese king is a half-blood -"

Like Noriak, Dossian thought, native blended with the ruling class.

"- and there's a lot of unrest. We could do good in both places, Doss." Her face shone, hungry with that desire. "We could change things."

He nodded for them to leave the tavern before something untoward happened. He didn't like some of the leers directed towards his beloved.

"I talked to someone," he said, "and -"

A strange resolve rose within him, and he decided before he could finish the sentence that he wouldn't tell her. He would do this on his own and bring the prize to her. Her world had collapsed: he would bring light into it with the unexpected reward. Noriak's request seemed plain enough, not too difficult – even for him.

"- I don't think I learned much," he finished. "Except that the Black Lords ... well ... they may be in contact with our academy."

It was as much improvisation as he could invent. Luckily, Callia took him at his word. "Really? Well, I had already figured we should head towards Varinhar. I won't fight the rhythmists, Doss – except to protect us, because I won't be stopped, either." The iron in her voice indicated she still thought she had done the right thing, even though people had died in the storms that crashed down on the Pass, even though a junior instructor had faced her and lost his life. She believed the Snowweavers – who lived on the opposite side of the Pass from the city of Trest – had murdered humans to suit their own ends, and before acting, she had gathered what was mostly proof.

Her conviction was enough for Dossian.

"South, then," he said.

They left Idiri and walked for two hours. When they stopped, Callia clapped out a straightforward rhythm to form a shelter barrier. They curled up under a tree.

She lay twined in his arms, a mote of a woman: he could have embraced two of her. "As long as I'm with you, Dossian, I'm home," she murmured.

He felt guilty he couldn't share the sentiment ... but the truth was, his mind ran wild with anxieties and ached for the familiar. He would follow her into anything, but that same devotion couldn't blow away the clouds.

"Love you," he said. It still felt like a failure as he closed his eyes.

***

The next morning, after a bit of cuddling and reluctance to move, the pair rose with grumbling stomachs. Nearby, they found a stream. Callia started a fire; Dossian managed to confuse a fish out of the water. Nuts and berries supplemented the meager meal, and they were on their way.

Callia established an ease-the-way spell, and the world welcomed them. Each step was smooth, each barrier or branch folding back without resistance. The wind never cut, nor the stones underneath their feet. The advantage to the spell was its subtlety: none of the farmers would notice anything strange about their presence, and it wouldn't disturb all but the strongest detection spells.

Not that they were being pursued yet. Ever, Dossian hoped.

Callia spoke of possible plans, not always to him, seeking a way forward with blind intensity. It started to sound more like revenge than justice, though he didn't dare point that out. She had meant the storms to punish the Snowweavers for their crimes, and had fallen short. She fell silent, and he squeezed her waist in place of words.

A golden hill came into view, pockmarked by stone. The ruins Noriak had told him about. Dossian felt his heart inch up his throat.

They encountered a farmer's path in the shadow of the hill. Dossian had a flash of inspiration.

"My stomach is already tingling," he said. "These outlying farms usually have more work than hands. If we could help them out with a few simple rhythms ..."

"Good idea," Callia said. They both had farming backgrounds and understood the march of monotony that kept a farm going. "We'll split up, cover more ground, and meet –" She scanned the horizon for a landmark.

He pointed to a massive oak. "There."

She grabbed him and kissed him. His head spun pleasantly, a taste better than any brandy. She bounded off in her chosen direction. Dossian watched her go, then heaved a deep breath and set out for the hill.

***

It turned out to be steeper than he had anticipated, and he wondered if the greatest risk he would face would be to his calf muscles. The ruins finally came into sight, an obliging materialization of shattered stone. One fifth of a fortress, sheltering a town that no longer existed. The construction reminded Dossian of the castles the Varinhese ruling class had imported from their more temperate motherland ... but was their regime old enough to have produced something so decrepit? He had no idea how long it took forts to fall into ruin and acquire desultory pieces of history.

Noriak had mentioned beasts. Dossian saw no evidence, no broken ground or track marks. Birds whirred in the trees. They stopped, disturbed, when he slung his small bowl-shaped drum down to tap out a protective pattern. It was an ordinary instrument used to supplement his skill. He was no master of barriers like Callia, but he could at least blunt the unwelcome teeth of any animal that lay within the ruins.

He searched the ruins. The old towers here, a blacksmith's shop there, and other remnants that could not even be clearly identified as buildings, much less their purpose. A human skeleton.

Dossian yelped and toppled backwards. Some kind of animal instinct suggested he should defend himself. He gathered his wits and studied it warily.

It seemed old, but how did one tell? He rose on shaky limbs and found another skeleton, then three more. Beyond that, a rotting tree trunk half-covered stone steps dropping into the earth. He approached, squinting down the mossy, leaf-littered staircase. Was this where he was meant to go?

He knew enough not to make a fool of himself shoving the trunk, even though there was no one to observe it. He drummed out a spell, feeling the vibrations as they shifted and then harmonized. The rotted wood tumbled out of the way.

Dossian drummed up a light-globe – one of the easiest apprentice spells – and peered down the steps. He could just see the bottom, a well of black. Swallowing, he picked his way down, one hand holding the globe, the other slipping along the slimy wall. His fingers sought cracks, but there were few. If he lost his footing, he would bounce down like a ball.

There had been a door at the bottom, presumably wood. The hinges and crossbars remained. A sour, stale aroma rose to meet him, tinged with – he sneezed – something musky. He held out the globe, casting spears of light across the floor.

Something bellowed its fury at being disturbed. He bolted backwards up the first four steps, clutching his drum. As he did, he lost his hold on the light-globe. It hovered on the landing.

Heart in his throat, Dossian waited for whatever it was to show itself. His fingers shuddered over the skin of the drum. Part of him yelped at the rest and wondered why he had been so foolish as not to tell Callia. What would it have hurt but his pride?

Something mahogany and indistinct loomed. It rippled, fuzzy under the globe's light. It lumbered into view: a giant bear with one ear missing and a baleful, squinting glare.

"Err ... sorry?" Dossian ventured.

The bear roared and charged to the bottom step. There it halted, hunched and waiting.

Just an ordinary bear, he realized, feeling foolish, and it was doing nothing more sinister than defending its comfortable, man-made cave. Unfortunately, he had to get past it. He backed up another few steps, shoulders tensed so hard the muscles protested.

He knew a sleep spell, and even though it wasn't hibernation season, it might be easier to use on a bear than a human. He began to drum.

The bear growled its protest, lunging up the first two steps. Dossian scampered backwards, losing the foundation of the rhythm.

"Everyone's a critic," he said. "All right. How about I just stand up here ..."

It seemed to take forever to reach the top step. He kept waiting for the bear to pursue him, but the massive mound of flesh and fur seemed only interested in defending its turf and not being subjected to pounding of a drum.

Once there, he steeled his nerves and began to tap, as softly as he could manage. Each beat was almost imperceptible, its contribution to the spell tiny ... but the bear seemed unbothered, though a low growl built in its throat when the interloper failed to depart.

Sweat pasted the back of his neck. It left its own beat on his spine. The vibrations of the spell built slowly. It was easier to tweak like this, easier to control – a precision he preferred, in place of talent he didn't have. Almost there ...

With a bellow, the bear thundered up the stairs. Dossian ground down on his panic. He abandoned the light taps and slammed down hard on the drum, ringing, resounding beats forcing the rhythm into completion.

The bear slowed, stumbling on a step. Dossian dove out of the way, somehow keeping hold of his drum as he somersaulted. He fetched up against the wall with a crack that sent shudders through his back, muted by his defensive spell. He bit his lip against the pain and repeated the last rhythm.

At the top of the steps, the bear turned, hunting irritably for the obnoxious human. It swayed and collapsed as it finished the turn.

Dossian breathed out, an unsteady snicker escaping him. Not the stuff epics were written about, but it had worked, and he was in one piece. He took a moment to check the latter fact, just for good measure.

Once satisfied, he rose and tapped out a continuance rhythm. He didn't want the bear to wake while he was below. Even knowing the spell was firm, he crept around the beast as much as possible, flinching when he had to nudge aside a hairy paw to reach the steps.

Down into the darkness, he rescued the light-globe and peered within, wary of cubs or a mate. Nothing moved. He found himself in a cellar. Time had destroyed its wares, leaving only shattered wine bottles and the remnants of animal inhabitants. He wrinkled his nose at the smell.

He sorted through the wreckage with his eyes first, hunting for anything that stood out. A rusted weapons rack stood in the back. He freed a decrepit sword from it and waved it about, but even he could tell the weapon was rusty beyond repair. He started to put it back when he noticed the silvery glint in the corner.

He dropped the sword with a clatter and knelt. He went to push aside cobwebs, but they had already been cleared from his goal. A chance swipe of the bear's paw, perhaps. The light-globe bobbed over his head. The object came to his hand before he saw it, the long bore of a flute. He pulled it out carefully, wary of breaking it.

It was made of silver, catching flickers of light. Untarnished, as brilliant as the day it had been made. It cast back red and blue against the yellow of the orb. The keys seemed to be in perfect shape.

He folded his fingers around the flute and felt faint vibrations moving through it. Not just any flute: enchanted, with a binding that had lasted centuries. It was older than the Varhinese occupation, had to be.

Dossian closed his eyes, feeling the primary vibration that moved through the flute. To anyone who didn't have the rhythmist sense, it would be still, but he couldn't read its purpose without a lengthy divination spell ... assuming he remembered how to cast it.

But he hadn't come here for the flute, precisely, only the money it would bring, though the thought of turning an unknown enchantment over to someone he barely knew made his stomach tighten. Lasting enchantments were rare, their art almost forgotten among modern rhythmists. This should go to one of the academies. It should ...

He shook himself. It wasn't as if he could deliver it. He and Callia were fugitives. He stroked the flute, resisting the impulse to play. As an inferior rhythmist, still bound to his drum while others needed nothing but their own bodies, he had developed an interest in other kinds of instruments. He had even picked up a few, before discovering he had even less talent with music.

He threaded the flute through his belt and rose. That had been easy – almost too easy. Couldn't Noriak have found a hunter to handle the bear? Dossian supposed he might not have known it was only a bear ... who would get close enough to a mysterious beast to find out, except one foolish rhythmist?

As he approached the landing, he dismissed the light-globe and the defensive spell. He stepped out into natural sunlight ... and stopped. Noriak stood at the head of the stairs, flanked by two men with crossbows. The great bulk of the bear loomed behind them, still slumbering.

The hair on the back of Dossian's neck prickled. "You didn't have to come all this way to meet with me," he said, feigning cheer.

"I did," Noriak said. "Hand over the flute."

"And you'll toss down the money?" Dossian said, dubious.

"No, I'm going to give you a better deal," Noriak replied. "Your life."

Dossian suppressed the urge to say it wasn't much of a deal, really, and his life could be compared unfavorably to that exchange of coins. "Why didn't you come for it yourselves?"

"You're a softhearted country boy, aren't you, Danth? Never had blood on your hands?"

Dossian realized the bear wasn't breathing. Shot in the heart, he guessed, and because of his spell, it wouldn't even have awakened. He felt as guilty as if he'd killed it himself.

"You shouldn't make assumptions about people," he said. "You don't know what I'm capable of."

Noriak indulged in laughter. "Yes, I do," he said. "I knew what you were the moment I saw you. That's why I called you over. That flute can't be taken by anyone who knows its true nature, unless given freely. If you don't hand it over, we kill you. You take the chance the next person might be as foolish as you. And the next. I'll get my hands on it soon enough. I've been hunting for this instrument for four years. I can wait."

"So you're thinking I'll feel guilty about the next person you fool?" Dossian asked. He decided that was as good a parting note as he was going to come up with, and hastily retreated into the cellar.

"What are you going to do, Danth?" Noriak called down. "Tunnel your way out?"

Dossian was wondering just that. He pulled out the flute, staring at it. What did it do? Could he leave it in the hands of someone willing to kill for it? Obvious why the cobwebs had been cleared: they'd come down here, discovered it, and either known it couldn't be removed or found out the hard way. And for a willing dupe, Noriak had chosen ... him. Anxiety and embarrassment twined around themselves in his mind.

"He could play it," a third voice said.

"Nonsense. Not unless he knows the right tunes. The odds of stumbling upon them by chance are astronomical. It took months of research ..."

Play it, Dossian thought in a rush, thanking them silently. They had no idea he was a trained rhythmist and could feel the vibrations that corresponded to the main tune. The only small problem was the fact he still had no idea what it would actually do.

He dithered, but if it was meant to do laundry or imitate an orchestra, the only thing that would happen was he would look foolish, and he was used to that. If it was meant to do something far more terrible ... better to unleash it now and know than to be left squirming, wondering what he had placed in Noriak's hands.

He lifted the flute to his lips and blew, moving his lips carefully until he identified the first note. He glided into the second, the third, and felt the beat. Four measures of three-four time, like a waltz.

He felt heartened by this. If it was a waltz, it couldn't possibly be that bad.

"Danth," Noriak shouted down, "you're messing with forces you don't understand -"

Though Dossian felt the vibrations building in the cellar, nothing happened until he concluded the last note. A tornado of pale blue light formed around him, swirling into a mass of mounted figures. Most of them seemed to be women; through his astonishment, Dossian noticed they were all lovely, though none as beautiful as Callia. He opened his mouth to ask a question.

The ghostly company surged into motion, some galloping up the stairs, others vanishing through the walls. It was soundless, all of it, not even the murmur of displaced air.

Then the shouting started.

Dossian pelted for the stairs, but by the time he reached the top, the struggle was over. The three men lay sprawled on the ground – unconscious, not dead, he was relieved to see – and the phantasmal parade stood at rest. When he came into the view, they turned to face him expectantly.

"Um, hi," he ventured. "Thank you for not killing them."

Their eyes shone in inverse, midnight to the fluorescence of their forms. They did not speak, remaining in a martial array. There seemed to be about thirty.

Dossian cleared his throat, toying with the flute. "Do any of you talk?"

There was no response. Dossian could imagine how the flute had come to be abandoned: a thief had taken it, not realizing its value, and the fort was attacked while such a valuable weapon lay in unsuspecting hands.

It was obvious the company must be controlled by the flute, but Noriak had been right: the odds of stumbling on the right combination of notes was astronomical. Dossian held up the flute and concentrated, but the only pattern he could feel was the one he had already played.

Still, on the off-chance that would reverse the process, he lifted it to his lips and played the tune again. The hordes stared dispassionately.

He shifted his attention to Noriak's slumped form. "Maybe you've got the music on you, since you seem to know so much about this," he pondered out loud. "I'd apologize for rifling through your pockets, but you did try to kill me." He felt somewhere between giddy and confused with his success. He had certainly earned it, but what to do from here?

"Dossian!"

He whirled towards the familiar voice. Callia stood on the edge of the ruins, eyes flared wide. The riders whirled like an avalanche to face her.

"Stand down," he yelped. "She's on our side."

To his relief, the ghostly warriors lowered their weapons. It seemed they did understand commands, as long as they were related to the purpose for which they had been summoned.

Callia flew through them without hesitation, a fiery blur. She hugged him tightly. "Are you all right? I saw the whirlwind of light ..."

"How did you get here so fast?" he asked.

"I used a variant of the dislocation spell," she said. "Short range."

He didn't respond. It had taken him weeks to memorize the long-range version, and he had been astonished when it worked.

"What happened, love?" she asked.

He told her the whole story, his cheeks flushing when he explained why he had made the agreement. "And this is the result," he said, holding up the flute. "It's ours now, I guess. I can't see turning it over to him."

She followed his gaze, her eyes hardening like lava. "Is that their leader?"

"Yes," he said, "that's Noriak -"

Callia swept over to the slumped figure, kicking him over with her foot. He spluttered in surprise, blinking into full consciousness. "Milady," he said, "what -"

Her palms rapped together, an invocation that slammed him into the ground. He cried into the earth. Callia twisted her hands, and the invisible force shoved him down harder.

"You threatened to kill my beloved," she said, her voice low and cold. "I'll show you the same courtesy."

Something cracked. Noriak howled. Dossian shook himself out of his stupor and shouted, "Stop!"

Callia's head snapped up. "This low-life doesn't deserve your sympathies, Doss. Are we going to leave him to scam someone else?" She slid her hands back together ...

But the blue brigade had heard him, and diaphanous hands reached down, pulling the tiny rhythmist away from the fallen man. She shrieked, in surprise as much as anything, but couldn't continue the spell. She twisted in their grip, teeth gritted. A low snarl started in her throat. He was stunned how animal it sounded.

"Callia, it's all right!" Dossian rushed forward, lifting his eyes to hers. "He's suffered enough. He's sure to think twice after this."

"Suffered enough?" The words were hoarse, lined with rage. Her eyes widened, but the wildness faded, and she saw him, really saw him. It seemed to take forever before she composed herself enough to speak again. "Dossian, he could have taken you from me, do you understand that?"

"I know." He cupped her chin, trying to keep his hand steady. "Let it go."

She bit her lip, nodded. "I trust you, Doss." Her voice was hoarse.

"You can let her go now," he said to the nearest warriors. He was relieved when they obeyed.

Noriak coughed, groaning, obviously oblivious to anything but his pain. "You're mad, both of you. Kill me, and you never get the tunes. I've got them memorized. Trapped here ..." He attempted to tap his temple, but couldn't wrest his arm up high enough.

"You've said it," Dossian said, hoping he sounded more confident than he felt. "Give us the tunes, and we'll go."

Noriak made a disgusted sound, but nodded. They had no paper; Callia had to craft some with a domestic spell. Noriak hummed, Dossian wrote, and the silent troops looked on.

There were ten other tunes, including a reversal. The company could build structures, fight, form an impenetrable barrier ... it was an impressive array.

Once Dossian had finished writing, Callia stared down at the Varinhese man. Her lips tightened, the primordial anger rising in her gaze. Dossian squeezed her arm, pulled her around to him – found in that moment, he was frightened, worried he couldn't calm her, worried what it would mean. He held her all the more tightly, willing his belief in her into the contact.

Wordless, she sighed and released the tension in her body. "Let's go," she said.

He lifted the flute to his lips and played the reversal tune. The company dissolved into mist. A faint halo of blue lingered ... then nothing.

They walked away.

***

Once the two rhythmists reached the bottom of the hill, Callia turned to him.

"You were amazing, Dossian," she said. "To lull the bear without hurting it – at risk to yourself – to bring the secret out of the flute ... and all this to protect me."

He shrugged, offered a sheepish smile. "It just sort of happened."

She laughed. "With you, it usually does. I wish I had your way of lucking into things."

She never ceased to astonish him, how she saw his shortcomings as hidden talents and believed in both. He realized had no regrets about leaving the academy behind, even though that would have been a quiet, sure life: a professional rhythmist, kept on retainer by a rich merchant or minor noble, with no worries, no doubts and no Callia. Hadn't he just shown he could muddle through, even when trapped? Confidence was a foreign thing to him, but he started to sense its edges.

Now, threaded through his belt, he had a whole new set of uncertainties. What would they do with the flute?

"Can I have it now?" she asked. "I think we're far enough away there are some experiments I would like to do."

His fingers curled around the flute to pull it free. He paused. He remembered the storms that had ripped through Neve Pass, heedless of whether their victims were human or Snowweaver, guilty or innocent. Her doing. He remembered the need in her face the day before, craving a fight. And the animal fury when she had confronted Noriak, wholly willing to break him.

Dossian loved her, but he had also learned a lot about her ... and realized, now, how much he still didn't understand. He had never liked mystery; now he hoped he could embrace it. He had promised, however privately, to protect her. That also meant from herself.

"I don't think we should play around with it just yet," he said. "I'll hang onto it, if you don't mind."

Callia gave him a quizzical look, then shrugged. "Fair enough. What we should focus on is putting distance between ourselves and Idiri, anyhow."

He tapped the flute, feeling the song at its soul. Mystery upon mystery ahead of them – but somehow, he would muddle through. "Varinhar awaits," he said.

Who?

By day, **George Anthony Kulz** writes software to transfer information from one computer to another. By night, he writes stories to transfer ideas from his imagination to the imaginations of others. He views both professions as a kind of magic.

Zachary Grant says: I study Biology at Queen's University, where I am a contributor to the school paper for reviews and flash fiction pieces. Apart from "Helios," I have another short story set for publication next spring with Rogue Planet Press– a speculative Lovecraftian mystery.

After retiring from a long and successful career as a software developer and technical architect, **David Castlewitz** turned to a first love: writing fiction, particularly SF, fantasy, magical realism, and light horror. His stories have appeared in many anthologies and online as well as print publications. David lives on the North Shore, outside Chicago, where he enjoys long walks, the occasional bike ride, and other outdoor adventures.

Visit his web site: http://www.davidsjournal.com to learn more.

A Jersey girl at heart, when **Lisa Voorhees** is not writing, she's usually listening to hard rock, bouldering, or sipping amaretto sours. Before she started writing novels, she earned her doctorate in veterinary medicine from Tufts University. Find out more about her at https://lisa.voorhe.es or http://facebook.com/lisavoorheesauthor . Interested in becoming a patron? Find out more about how to support her creative work and receive bonus material at http://www.patreon.com/lisavoorhees .

www.ingramcontent.com/pod-product-compliance
Lightning Source LLC
LaVergne TN
LVHW012028060526
838201LV00061B/4515